Lillian's Last Affair

and other stories

by Sue Katz

Published by

Consenting Adult Press

Arlington, MA 02474

ISBN: 978-0-9913122-1-4

consentingadultpress@hotmail.com

ACKNOWLEDGEMENTS

Dedicated to Flo Hochman (1928 – 2014)

Since I lack a writing "room of my own," I mostly worked on these stories when house-sitting around the country and abroad at the homes of my generous friends Tracy, Sue O, Susan, Stephanie, Lisa, Judy, Jaya, Gilbert, Eleanor, Dolita, Clint, and others. My readers have saved my butt repeatedly, so thanks to Barry, Bess, Donna, Flo, Gema, Gina, Jaya, John, Leslie, Lily, Sandy, Schweid, Verandah, and many others.

The elders in my fitness classes were my inspiration, and Barry my muse.

I called on several professionals. Barbara Mende was my invaluable copyeditor. Ken Wachsberger was my book buddy – and beat me to it. Gina Ogden prodded me forward. We are all members of the National Writers Union.

Sandy Oppenheimer, the collage artist, posed for the cover photo and John Fischer, the sculptor, took the photo. Deborah Bernard encapsulated the vision for my cover.

Thanks to Cal Sharp of Caligraphics for swift formatting and design, and clear guidance. www.caligraphics.net

WHAT OTHERS ARE SAYING ABOUT *Lillian's Last Affair*

Buckle your seatbelt for an exhilarating ride. Lillian, Ruby, and other habitants of Sue Katz's deeply irreverent stories… are touching, shining, tawdry, and sometimes hilarious.

--Gina Ogden, PhD, LMFT, author of *Women Who Love Sex* and *The Return of Desire*

Sue Katz's deftly understated narrative authority and the descriptive bull's eyes… astonish us page after page. Brava!

--Steve Windwalker, bestselling author and founder of *BookGorilla.com* and *Kindle Nation*

Sue Katz's stories are full of pleasure, pain, and humor, with carefully drawn, superbly evoked characters.

--Richard Schweid, Oscar-nominated documentarian and author of *Che's Chevrolet*

Sexy, poignant, funny, [and] raw… Sue Katz makes us think – and makes us feel.

--Joan Price, award-winning author of *Naked at Our Age*

Sue Katz tackles the heart-wrenching challenges that the elderly and disabled face each day – subjects that few writers are brave enough to acknowledge.

--Gloria Brame, Ph.D., author and world-renowned sex therapist

ABOUT THE AUTHOR

Sue Katz is a wordsmith and rebel who has lived and worked on three continents: first as a martial arts master, then promoting transnational volunteering, and currently teaching fitness and dance to seniors and elders. Her fiction and non-fiction have been published for decades in anthologies, magazines, and online. She spent several years shining *Lillian's Last Affair* - a true labor of love. She wrote the book *Thanks But No Thanks: The Voter's Guide To Sarah Palin* in 28 days and nights. You can reach her at consentingadultpress@hotmail.com.

TABLE OF CONTENTS

Lillian’s Last Affair

"So we've burned ourselves," the nurse's condescending tone invaded the room. "Now wasn't that foolish!"

Lillian longed to smile her most old lady-ish smile and answer, "Fuck you." It was one of her private pleasures, something she practiced in a conversational tone on crowded buses when she was jostled, or in the aisle of the supermarket when a harried younger person carelessly bumped his backpack into her head. She liked to say it to the television set when some comedian was ridiculing immigrants or fat people or, for that matter, the disabled. Why hadn't they found a funny comedian since George Carlin died? George also liked to say Fuck. This patronizing nurse, though, probably wouldn't even believe her own ears if Lillian said it out loud. At 84 Lillian was invisible.

The doctor had been an ass as well.

"I'm afraid, Mrs. Letzburg . . ." he had started.

"Call me Lillian, please." She might as well have kept her mouth shut, for all he took notice. She had tried to establish eye contact, but he had been looking over her shoulder. When she twisted to see what he was staring at, there was only a clock on the wall and a diagram of some dissected organ.

"I'm afraid that there is little we can do about your peripheral neuropathy. But we will certainly help you with the burns on your feet. From now on, you do understand, you have to test the bath water before stepping into it. Nice seeing you. I'll send in the nurse to dress those burns."

He had left Lillian alone in the cubicle once again. She had already waited so long for Dr. Lin to arrive that she had finished an entire issue of the Computer Weekly magazine that happened to be lying near her in the examining room. Once he spent his obligatory five minutes looking at her burns, barely touching her, he was gone. Lillian was left wondering if it would be the nice nurse or the brusque one.

"From now on, dear" – that obnoxious *dear* brought Lillian back to the present – "you'd better use your elbow as a temperature tester, not your feet." And how exactly, Lillian wondered, am I to reach the water with my elbow? "Those feet of yours don't work very good. Oh well, let's get some goop on those tootsies."

Exercising her strongest self-restraint, Lillian just managed to refrain from punctuating that juvenile word "tootsies" with a "Fuck you."

It seemed unfair to suffer from two chronic conditions. First there was the neuropathy, which was increasingly crippling her, with one foot turned out at a distorted angle and the leg withering away.

And then there was the way people had been treating her like a child ever since she became white-haired and gimpy. She knew she would be unable to shake off either of these conditions until the day she died, no matter how many times she cussed at them. Piss off, she often hissed at her uncooperative foot. Piss off, she spat at her age spots, at her ingrown toenails, at the roll of quarters that had disappeared yesterday, never to be found.

The nurse told her to switch from baths to showers, but she and Bernard had never had a shower put in. That would change when she finally sold the house and moved into a senior condo. Then she'd have a modern shower with grab bars and people to call in dangerous situations. Then she'd have a bit of peace and quiet, not worrying about the leak in the roof or those horrible ants that had colonized her garden. An elevator would replace the steep steps to her front door. If she could afford Manor House, she'd be able to sit with Lenny and Freda – or Sarah, for that matter – for meals. They could discuss the news sensibly, exchange books, share a cab to the films.

The cream applied and her feet bandaged, Lillian was sent to the pharmacy one floor down to await her ointment prescription. She glanced at her oversized digital watch – an ugly thing that made her feel she was wearing a microwave on her wrist, but a thoughtful gift from her grandson Leon – and saw that she had 25 minutes to wait for The Ride to come back and get her – assuming, and it was probably an overly optimistic assumption, that it would arrive at the agreed time.

She thought of the overworked driver trying to nurse that old van along. How the hell do they expect gimps and crips, as a paraplegic friend liked to say, to get anywhere in this city? She was tempted to shake her fist at the sky and yell, Eat Shit! That's one her granddaughter Lisa had schooled her in; Lisa liked to keep Lillian's potty mouth up-to-date. But she was in the line for the pharmacy and everyone around her seemed miserable enough already. Instead of yelling, she settled on a bench next to a young mother who looked shattered. The woman was trying to hold her squirming daughter still by clutching her between her knees so that she could tidy a couple of the many beaded braids that decorated the toddler's head. A little boy was on the bench on the woman's other side, attempting to climb onto her lap by gripping her poor stretched-out sweater as an anchor.

Lillian considered helping out – perhaps diverting the attention of the little boy, but she didn't want to risk him stepping on her singed feet. Anyway, she had well and truly paid her dues. First Norman and then later Michael had been a handful in her day, the years following the war. After her husband Bernard had returned from Brussels, where he had spent a lot of his war, he had gone from one traveling sales job to another while he tried to figure out how he was going to support his family, leaving Lillian with two children in a tiny two-bedroom apartment over the real estate office that often brought up typing piecework for her to do while the boys were, theoretically, napping.

"If it wasn't for the G.I. Bill," Lillian thought about Bernard going to college, "we would've had a much different life. Bernard would never have become an engineer or invented that air vent. On the other hand, he wouldn't have been able to afford that old Ford for Norman and he might be alive today." She didn't have time to get sad because they called her to the window to pick up her ointment.

"Cream and wrap in gauze twice a day," the pharmacist said, "morning before you put on your socks and then night before bed. And put on a clean pair of socks for the night." She signed, she nodded, and she headed for the elevator to go downstairs where, after many requests, the clinic had set up a bench inside the exit door for elders to wait for their rides. Of course it had taken more than requests. It had taken a little handwritten petition that Lillian had convinced a half-dozen folks to sign.

The next morning, after creaming her feet and wrapping them in gauze as instructed, Lillian dressed and emailed her friends at Manor House to make sure she was still invited for lunch. She had to leave pretty early to navigate the bus to the train and then the shuttle from the station, but she brought along a book for the down times.

"Then that is that," Freda said during dessert, "you'll find yourself a vay to fit into a von-bedroom like I am doing. Lenny, is there not a von on mine floor? Bertrise died, may her name be a blessing, and their daughter Deshawna is moving her dad into a nursing home, the poor man. End of the month, no? Didn't Deshawna go to school mit your Michael?"

"No, not Michael," Lillian said and Freda dropped that point and went on. "Think on it, you'd be just the other end of the hall from me. But don't be vorrying. I vouldn't be knocking your door every minute and you vouldn't be knocking mine, so ve vouldn't have, as they say, no invasions of piracy." Freda's friends had long ago stopped pointing it out when she mixed up a word.

But Sarah and Lillian exchanged an indulgent look over Freda's head, that subtle, charming smile stretching Sarah's lips, smoothing out those tiny wrinkles around her mouth. Already Lillian had secrets with Sarah. She had met her through Freda and Freda's brother Lenny, old friends from the peace movement who had moved together into Manor House. Sarah was a broad-shouldered woman of 79, a retired librarian, her salt and red pepper hair in two long braids down her straight back. She wore tie-dyed oversized tees and jeans and was never without a couple of books in her hands and a pair of sparkly-framed reading glasses on her nose.

They hadn't talked much alone, but they shared a growing attachment. Every time Lillian was in Sarah's company she had an inexplicable sense of anticipation – as if happiness were right around the corner. She found herself shivery and hot at the same time, especially when Sarah patted her hand during conversations. By the fourth or fifth time they all had lunch together, Lillian recognized what was going on for her – she had simply never experienced it over a woman before – and it made her all that more eager to join their community. The next time Sarah touched her hand at the table, Lillian had squeezed and held on to it for just a moment. It was a game-changer for them both, punctuated by a mutual glance of recognition. Time, though, was the ultimate matchmaker. if I'm going to go after one more affair of the heart at 84, Lillian thought, I'd better get my ass in gear.

Freda took Lillian down to the office where the personable saleswoman was always available, especially now that the real estate mess was keeping people from selling their homes and the recession had shrunk the seniors' life-long investments. Manor House had plenty of empty units. Lillian talked to the young woman for more than 20 minutes, filled out the application, and left with brochures galore and a lightness of heart she hadn't felt since Bernard was still alive.

She was sick of responsibility, sick of caring for precious knick-knacks that were precious to no one else, sick of handling everything on her own, sick of feeling guilty every time she looked at the weedy yard. Most of all, she was sick of schlepping down to the bus stop to pick up a free newspaper because she didn't want to pay for a subscription to the daily. "You're house poor," Michael had said. "You're camped out in the middle of the only money you have – the equity of this home." All those nice investments Bernard made: this market collapse killed them. But Lillian didn't believe that "collapse" was the right word. She preferred to say "theft." Those bankers, those Wall Street thieves, screw them!

If she sold the house, though, she could afford Manor House. It meant stripping down – things and worries – and she was more than ready. It meant the end of her isolation – physically, emotionally, and even politically.

Back home she looked around. She saw the large, upholstered furniture, a million years old, but still well taken care of. She saw the big walnut dining table with the six matching chairs that Bernard had bought on credit when he was starting out so that they could entertain his boss without shame. She wandered past the sewing room with her treadle machine and ironing board. She'd miss having a sewing machine, although she hadn't touched it in years. Maybe her granddaughter Lisa would want it. She wouldn't miss the dusty three-legged ping-pong table in the basement or Bernard's war mementos, rotting in an olive green army trunk in the attic.

"I'll dump it all," she thought happily. "I'll give it all to charity. I'll just keep my red armchair and then buy some cheap scaled-down furniture. I only need a few pieces: a love seat, a table for four, a bed, a bureau. And while I'm at it, I'll get new towels."

The doorbell rang and then she heard the door open. Had she forgotten a visit from her granddaughter? "Who is it?" she called from upstairs.

"It's Michael and Emily." Lillian was puzzled, checked her massive watch. It was too early for Michael, who should be at work.

She made her way downstairs, carefully, step by step, both feet to each step. Now that she had definitely decided she would move to Manor House, she sure as hell didn't want the neuropathy to trip her up.

"I'm coming, dears."

They were sitting on the couch, glum, nervous.

Michael picked at his ear as he had done since adolescence, since they'd lost Norman. Emily, her hair in an especially sloppy ponytail, looked beseechingly at him, a pose that irritated Lillian.

Divorce? A kid in trouble?

"Tea? Something to eat?"

"Sit down, Ma. I'm afraid it's bad news."

Michael had lost his job. Emily had been laid off months and months ago, but they hadn't minded so much. They expected the adopted kid from China to arrive soon, so she would need to be home anyway. But Michael's job was supposed to be secure. Like his father before him, he was an engineer. He had been working for AT&T for years, but had moved to what he called a "start-up" just over a year ago because they'd doubled his salary.

"The rumor is that the CFO ran off with the funds. And it's just a couple weeks before the company was going to go public." Lillian more or less followed his explanation. "I would've made a killing if it had gone public. Instead, the place closed and there's an investigation. I've been taking half my salary in stock from the start, to, you know, build a nest egg – now it's worthless. We aren't even sure we can pay rent next month. The trips to China and the fees and the downturn – they've wiped out our savings." This was like an echo from the TV, from the papers. All the news was about losing houses and jobs and futures. Lillian and her friends took this all very personally. After all, they had paid their dues, they had survived one Depression. Why should they be subjected to another?

"I'm afraid, Ma, that I have to ask you if you would let us move the family in here with you. We don't really have a lot of other options. If you really think about it, you'll see it's a good thing. We can look after you and you can help with the kids and that will give you something to do. You love your grandkids, right?"

Lillian felt nauseous. Michael had always been a would've-should've guy, but now he felt perfectly willing to plot out her old age, without consulting with her. The idea of the four of them moving in just in time to receive another adopted kid was more than she could bear. She'd flee to Manor House and leave them the house. But she couldn't afford Manor House unless she sold the house. It was times like this that she wished she believed in some god or other, because damn it she would be praying. Instead she felt sick, her feet suddenly flamed, and she wished her kids would leave. At least that wish came true quickly. Michael and Emily must have assumed she'd love their plan and when they saw her stark dejection, they left in confusion.

She called the nice young woman at Manor House the next morning, followed by the realtor, and put it all on hold. She then called Freda, who scolded her and chided her and said that it was a bit late in life to become a mortar. "Martyr," Lillian corrected before she could stop herself. "Vatever," said Freda with real sadness. Lillian counted on Freda to pass the bad news to Lenny and, more importantly, to Sarah.

For the next three weeks she exhausted herself trying to prepare the house for the approaching tsunami of relatives and their possessions. She had expected to have to sort out a lifetime of acquisitions, but only in anticipation of a move she longed to make. Now it was a bitter chore, not one that held out hopes for a life she wanted. Like so many other people, she was suffering from recession depression – and from the need to abandon her dreams in the face of duty. Fuck you, J.P. Morgan, she muttered as she packed away box after exhausting box of her past. Fuck you, Bank of America.

And then her son's family arrived, transforming her home into an emotional zoo. Michael was deeply guilt-ridden that he had left a steady job for something so fleeting and Emily was almost blindly happy about the impending arrival of the three-year-old Chinese girl. Because of the sudden move, Lillian's granddaughter Lisa had been ripped from tentative handholding with her 15-year-old neighborhood boyfriend, and her grandson Leon had lost his high-school baseball team. Not only were these two already burdened with adapting to a new school, they were also trying to work out how they were going to share the attic – and share their parents, once the Chinese sibling arrived. They put up a room divider Lillian took from the laundry room and pushed two chests of drawers back to back down the middle of the room, but both kids knew it was the end of privacy – just in the middle of their teen years, awash in hormones and self-consciousness.

Lillian's days were completely overrun by the bereft, moody children, while her nights were wrecked by Michael's decision to take the bedroom next to hers for him and Emily. Lillian had assumed that the new little girl would be put there. It made her feel squeamish to hear them talking in bed and even more uncomfortable when she heard grunts instead of words. Lillian's ears became annoyingly hypersensitive, as if they had turned into TV satellite dishes, picking up all the noise of her son and daughter-in-law's sex life. Her peace of mind was shattered and her old age was being ruined by four ultra-needy relatives.

The situation got worse once Emily left for China to pick up the adoptive sister. Michael was out all the time, doing what they call "networking" to improve his job search. But there weren't any jobs – that was the point, wasn't it? The economy was down the drain and her family was sucking

Lillian down it too.

Lillian felt like a prisoner in Guantanamo. Her independent life as a widow had been abruptly snatched from her and now she had to do what others told her to do. The grandchildren interrogated her ruthlessly – What would the toddler from China be like? When could they go back to their old school? Could they visit their friends in their real neighborhood? Why couldn't they have this video game or that pair of tennis shoes? Their home, their friends, their school, and most of all their parents had evaporated unexpectedly. Lillian felt the same: her own true life had been obliterated. She seemed to be serving a life sentence with no appeal – and how much more life could she count on? Was it worth being docile with the clock ticking and possible sweetness dangling just out of reach?

Freda was a good friend. Just as she had done when Bernard first passed away, Freda called her each and every day to remind her that there was a whole world out there and that people loved her. Unlike Michael and Emily, Freda asked about Lillian's health during every call and listened patiently to stories of how the children ran past her as she ascended the stairs step-by-step, throwing her off balance. Of how her son resented it when she went off to long medical appointments.

Freda often ended their conversations with a message from Sarah – perhaps an invite to a film evening or an offer to come over to Lillian's place for tea. But that was out of the question.

The house had become a chaotic jumble, especially while Emily was abroad for nearly a month closing the adoption. Lillian had slowed down, gingerly moving around her own home in fear that she'd trip on a abandoned school book or slip on a discarded sock. Michael was either out or depressed in front of a TV sports show – brushing away the children when they tried to get his attention and picking at his ear 'till it bled. When Emily returned with their new kid, it got much worse. The three-year-old frequently banged her head against the wall, a not unknown symptom of orphanage children, and had breathing problems that led to piles of vomity washcloths strewn around. Emily ignored her older kids in the face of the needs and novelty of this child. Absent any parent, Lisa and Leon clung even more desperately to Lillian. She felt like the woman in the pharmacy that day she had waited for the burn cream: small people trying to climb up and colonize her. Lillian loved her grandkids, but she had had plans – she had had a future and very little time to wait. Fuck this shit, she finally decided.

Once Emily was settled back in, Lillian announced that she was going to lunch with her friends across town and that she would be doing so at least weekly. For a moment Emily flashed a look of surprised disappointment, but quickly returned to her blissful if selective mothering. Michael had more or less absconded. How much networking could one engineer do?

It had been a long time since she'd taken the bus to the train and the shuttle to Manor House, but Lillian didn't remember it as quite so dragged out or such a strain on her bad leg. She was impatient to see her friends. Sarah and she had developed a rich email connection and the truth was that their frequent, flirtatious correspondence was Lillian's greatest if not her only secret pleasure, now that her own privacy was so compromised with her son in the next bedroom.

At first, Sarah had only sent her political petitions to sign or muckraking articles to read. But then one day Sarah wrote, "I'm sending you this petition, but what I'd really like to send you is a big hug. Not only because you seem to be having such a tough time, but because I need a hug from you."

Lillian wrote back, "I'd love to send you an email hug, but I think our first real hug should be in person. I need to escape from here and come see you."

Sarah answered, "Yes! We need to be face-to-face, with candles, music, wine."

And that's when Lillian had made the decision to end her 24/7 imprisonment with a visit to her friends. As the shuttle let her off in the driveway of

Manor House, she could see Freda and Lenny pressed up against the glass of the front doors. Approaching, she saw that Sarah was standing right behind them, her neat braids hanging over her handsome shoulders. In the midst of a welcome home that rivaled that of a returning soldier, Lillian finally got her hug, in person, with Sarah. As their chests and tummies came together, their arms wrapped around each other's back, the noise and the gaiety and the celebratory motion all faded. A charged silence seemed to surround them for an embrace that was to change so much.

"Let's have us some tea," Freda said with excitement. "Come to my room." Sarah grabbed Lillian's hand for a hidden squeeze as the four of them tumbled into the elevator. It was wonderful to be with peers again, and titillating to be carrying on a flirtation right under the noses of dear friends and relatives.

There were homemade cakes and hot tea. Lenny poured, as always maintaining a soft space in the background while Freda chattered. "Nu, how's by the crazy family? Why can't you move here and leave those *schlumpers* at your house?"

"I can't buy here without selling the house and I can't sell the house when my own family has nowhere to live."

"Guess what. We have such an idea, no Lenny?"

Lenny nodded with a smile.

"Next month we needs go to Florida to see our cousins. She is qvite ill with the diabetes; they need help, some company. They have them a big house, so ve're going for at least six veeks. Why shouldn't you move in here to our place and see what you see." Freda turned towards a surprised and hopeful Sarah. "Sarah vould look after you here, no?"

"Oh, I couldn't," Lillian said automatically, and then whipped around to lock eyes with Sarah. "Or could I?"

When she announced at the dinner table back home that she was going to Manor House for six weeks, the outrage and fear was palpable. "But Ma," Michael whined, "we need you here. With the three kids and everything...."

"These are not my children, Michael. These are your children with Emily and I wish you all the best of luck. But by my 85th birthday I should be able to do more with my life than babysit. Not that I don't love you all. I do. But I have a shot at some happiness and I'm going to take it."

She stood up from the table. Lisa and Leon looked with confusion from their parents to their grandmother. Emily and Michael were incredulous. "But Mother," Emily said, "What could be more joyous than family?" How Lillian, looking around at the chaos, wanted to say, "Are you fucking kidding me?" Instead she said, "Well, sex with a new lover, for one."

She limped to her room to email Sarah. "Mission accomplished. Get the hot water bottles ready for my leg and an extra tube of Bengay for your back. I'll bring the candles and wine."

Ruby's Path to the Sea

"I'd be glad to show you the beach," Ruby says, adjusting the pink sparkle headband over her grey roots.

"Why, thanks for the offer, but I'm not sure I've got the time. I've got an early evening class back in Boston." I am packing up my iPod and my music equipment after teaching a one-off fitness class in this Marshfield subsidized senior housing estate. Ruby has remained behind after the other students dispersed.

"It's only a mile away," she says to my back, following me as I carry my gear to my car.

Why not, I think. It would be nice to see the ocean. I clear the half-empty potato chip bag and the talking books off the passenger seat. "Shall we?" I say to this stranger, with a chivalrous sweep of my arm. The old woman giggles, gets in without difficulty, and I buckle her in.

"Take a left," she says imperiously, chin held high – teacher's pet – as we pass out of the housing development. She is hoping that the others see her leaving with me. It's a sad life when I'm the celebrity of the day.

We proceed down to the end of the uneven street, lined with a few scraggly trees, passing a larger housing project that looks like barracks. I assume it houses families. “Take a left,” she says again, and I turn onto a two-lane road. We drive past several rickety private homes, a car repair shop, and then a large one-story concrete box building that looks like it was abandoned years ago. “I met my husband Carl at this roller skating rink,” Ruby says, and then with some urgency, “Take this right!”

I brake, signal, and turn all at once and luckily there seem to be no other cars in the tri-state area to pose a threat. “I just wanted you to see the parking lot, on this side,” she explains, “because this is where Carl gave me my first kiss. I mean my first kiss ever. He was my one and only, you see. We had just done a beautiful waltz on the skates – they always played a last waltz on Saturday night – and I guess there was a certain feeling between us. He was known as the best dancer in town – even on skates – and I was no slouch either, so there was every reason to be together. We were both 16. He must’ve had his license for about three weeks and already his dad was giving him the car on Saturday night. My girlfriends were jealous.”

She falls into a solemn quiet.

“Where to?” I nudge. She shivers and then says, “Make a U-turn and continue on the main street.” I’ll be damned if I can see any street one could, in good conscience, call “main,” but I return to the road we had been on.

We ride in silence for a few minutes, until Ruby tells me to take the next right and then another right immediately after that. I'm in a small dead-end street and just two doors down she points at a triple-decker. "That was the first place we lived, up there on the third floor. It had attic ceilings so Carl could never stand up straight, which was a problem when he was getting dressed for work. He was a security guard in those first years, and they had him decked out to look like a cop. He always complained that the attic was giving him bad posture."

"How nice of you to tell me about Carl." I don't actually know how to respond to this unanticipated autobiographical tour. "So is this place close to the sea?" I hope that a gentle reminder of our destination might be timely.

"About a mile," she answers.

Three or floor blocks on, Ruby says, "Bear left here. We'll take a shortcut." Soon we approach a largely abandoned parade of shops, where she motions me to pull up. A liquor store is still operating and has a few cars parked in front of it, and next to it is a boarded-up fruit and vegetable shop. "Thirty-two years," Ruby says. "Thirty-two years Carl and I got up at 4:00 to go to the Haymarket stalls to pick up the fresh produce. I used to worry about the farmers from Maine and New Hampshire and Western Mass who brought their crops – what time did they get up? Anyway, we were very well known in this area. Honest. Not playing with the scales. Fresh daily. We made a decent living here, although you'd never know it now from looking at the place." The sign was faded, but I could make out "Carl's Produce" surrounded by dim images of dancing grapes and lettuce and potatoes.

"When you're getting up at that hour more or less every day," Ruby laughs, "you've got a different life from everyone else. It means you're in bed by 8:00. Carl couldn't be in the Marshfield Veterans' bowling league even though he was wicked good at it. We couldn't go dancing, and that broke my heart. It was like the whipped cream was removed from our romance. Because we worked on the weekends, too. People come to depend on you. They need something, they say to themselves, 'Carl's.' So if you're closed, they might think about going somewhere else. Did I mention that we never had kids?"

I turn my head her way and we make direct eye contact for the first time, but her eyes are cold. "No we didn't. There wasn't time. I used to dill the pickles myself, barrels of them, and my pickled tomatoes were a hit. I baked the Sunday morning coffee cakes – I could always sell more than I made." She nods my way with a satisfied grin, as if in recognition of loud applause. I try to smile towards her but her gaze quickly returns to her old storefront.

"I was relieved when we made enough to hire someone to go with Carl to the Haymarket in the mornings, then I was able to make a lot more homemade items for the shop. By that time we had bought a television for our living room in our own house, so I'd watch the morning programs while I separated out portions of dates, wrapped them in plastic, and then sealed them using my iron. My fresh pasta was a major hit. Later I bottled up my marinara sauce. Of course this is before the days of so much instant food. In those days you could get frozen TV dinners and pot pies, but if you didn't want to be embarrassed to be serving ready-made to your own flesh and blood, you came to Carl's for Ruby's food."

I don't know how to get us back in gear, as it were, so I mumble, "It sounds like you and Carl were very hard-working folks," and start pulling out of the parking lot back onto the road, without her instructions.

"Hard-working?" Ruby chewed on my phrase a bit and smoothed out her skirt. "Our hours were long, that's for sure, but I don't know as the work was all that hard. I had a brother in the mines in West Virginia. I'd call that hard work. Of course dragging out the stands once Carl was back from Haymarket was a bit back-breaking, then piling up the goods in pyramids that wouldn't topple if some kid looked at them cross-eyed, now that was a skill."

I'm getting to like Ruby and I realize that she probably doesn't have much access to a car, so this stroll down memory's lanes might be a rare opportunity. On the other hand, I've got to head back to town in time. "Which way to the sea, Ruby?"

"You're doing fine. Take your first left." I did as she said, but that took me onto a residential road of postwar bungalows that curved more or less around back of the parade of shops where she and Carl had worked. Some of the houses had add-ons, like apartments over the garage or landscaped gardens, and others were sagging and peeling.

"Slow up," Ruby lightly puts her hand on my thigh to get my attention. "See the one with the blue trim? That was our house for 28 years – although the trim was brown in our day. Look, they've kept all my bushes. Got a new awning over the front porch, though." The house is still in its original form, a two-bedroom, I estimate. "Carl hadn't really wanted a bungalow when we were looking for a house because he didn't think the ceilings would be high enough and he was sick of hunching over in the attic apartment. But the ceilings were just fine, except that they had swirly patterns that got on our nerves after a few years. And in the end he was glad not to have stairs to climb, after carrying all those crates around wore his back out.

"I didn't like the paneling. So fake looking. I personally would have gone for wallpaper. A girlfriend of mine about that time put this whole mural of a lake surrounded by wooded mountains on the back wall of her dining room where there weren't any windows. So when you ate at her place, you felt like you were out in the wilderness. I really wanted something like that. She said there were other murals – even one that had a window and curtains painted on it and you could look through and see a farm. That would've been a laugh. But Carl wasn't one to put money into a house, especially when we weren't in it all that much, so we never changed anything."

I keep driving. "Well, wait one darned minute." I think she wants me to stop but she keeps talking and I realize she is basically speaking to herself anyway. "That isn't true. He made one change when we moved in – a big change. There were two bedrooms, one right after the other. He decided to make them into one big room. He had the wall knocked down and at least I got a big wall closet out of the change. I understood his point of view. We knew we weren't going to have children, so he said that since the bedroom was his favorite room in the house, he'd prefer it to be the largest room. My Carl. He did like to be in the bedroom." She stops and seems to be waiting for me to say something, but I'm at a loss.

"With me," she adds with pride, prompting me.

"Sounds like a close marriage," I respond.

"If you're going to be with someone 24 hours a day, working and living and working some more, you better have an activity you like to share outside the shop. That was our activity. You know. He wouldn't let me pull down the plastic wood paneling and put up a mural, but I can't tell you how many new beds he kept buying. First was our double bed – we stayed in that for years. Then he got a Queen-sized and I bought my first fitted sheets – they were lemon yellow. In the late 70s he bought a water bed but to tell the truth that didn't work so well for us because it was hard to get in it and out of it and it's hard enough to get up at 4:00, let alone feeling all seasick."

Ruby goes all quiet. "No, that waterbed was a mistake. A big one. It can ruin all the carpets from the water pouring out." She looks at me, "That happened to us. Do you want to hear what happened?"

I nod as I glance at the clock on the dashboard. I thought this whole excursion was going to take me 15 or 20 minutes and then I could beat rush hour back to town for my next group. As it is, 40 minutes have gone by already and I don't know if we're closer or farther from the ocean than when we started.

"Here's what happened. I was down in the store alone because Carl was off to the Milford farm to get apples from the Polish farmer. My stomach was acting up and I had to use the ladies. I didn't want to use the store toilet in this situation, if you know what I mean, so I asked Mrs. Green, my neighbor, to watch the store while I ran down the street to our house, where I'd have more privacy, not worry about noises. I come in the door and I can hear the waterbed sloshing around. I mean, how could that be? Sloshing around on its own?"

I pull the car over into a driveway as soon as I hear her voice catch and realize that Ruby's face is wet with tears. I twist in my seat so that she has my full attention, although I can't pretend I'm not getting concerned about the time. I'm feeling trapped and sympathetic all at once. Life never gives you a chance to feel just one pure emotion at a time. "I think maybe it's broke. Or the neighborhood kids got in. Or maybe a burglar. I tiptoe down the hall, picking up a big knife as I go through the kitchen, and I can hear voices. Not so much voices as sounds. The bedroom door is shut – both of them were – because we still had the two doors left over from when it was two rooms. I pull open the door and find them. Carl was with Marie. She's sitting on top of him, bouncing, laughing."

As soon as she says "Marie," I know just who

she's talking about. Another one of the students in the class was named Marie. I had noticed her for two reasons. She came to fitness wearing high-heels and a wide black patent leather belt around a giraffe-patterned tunic. That makes you stand out during exercises. And during class the two of them openly squabbled. Ruby had fetched paper cups for our drink breaks from the supply closet and Marie had said, "For god's sake. Those are for coffee, not water." Her vehemence had made an impression on me.

"I lost my mind. Marie, the slut. My biggest enemy from high school. The homecoming queen with the tight sweaters and no curfew and she's already been through three husbands. Why does she need my husband too? I hardly remembered I had the knife in my hand and Carl was screaming at me, Ruby, Ruby, and before I knew it I had sliced the waterbed three or four times and the water was almost up to my ankles."

In the excitement of reliving her nightmare, Ruby's headband has fallen down to the bridge of her nose, the tip of which is dripping as she sobs. She digs out an embroidered handkerchief to blow her nose and wipe her face, before pushing the headband back up where it belongs. She waves her hand vaguely in the direction to the right and I understand that I am to continue driving.

We're quiet for a few minutes and then, as we

pass a cemetery, she points out her window. "There's Carl." She hardly wastes a glance in his direction. As I drive on it seems to be getting darker and darker and I realize that it is seriously clouding over. At last the road merges into the seaside drive and I pull in to a parking area. We get out of the car – finally I am to see this panoramic view that so distinguishes Marshfield according to its residents. But as we lean over the sea wall, all we see is fog. If I lean way over, I can see some wet rocks below, but otherwise it's just a soupy curtain.

"Well, it's often foggy down here," Ruby says, "but when it's clear, it's very nice. Can I go home now?"

There's nothing to see so I follow her back to the car and she says, "Just drive straight from here. In one mile it turns into the street you'll recognize where our development is. I hate that place. I didn't used to. Not until they moved Marie down the hall from me. Now I don't have a moment's peace."

We Don't Say Such Things Out Loud

On his 80th birthday, Frank nearly got turned on to smoking by his son FJ – that's Frank Junior – and his daughter-in-law Juliet. He had never smoked a cigarette in all his life and considered it a stinky, nasty habit – one he unfortunately had to live with. For nearly 60 years his wife Catherine and he had been playing a tedious game. They'd finish a meal at a restaurant. She'd smile coquettishly and say that she had to go to the powder room to touch up her lips. She'd sweep across the room carrying her handbag, usually something in plastic that matched the color of her shirtwaist dress, her insincere theatrical smile about to receive a strong layer of orange or red lipstick. Five minutes later she'd come back in a haze of Woolworth's brand of toilet water, rubbing perfumed lotion into her hands, and chewing Juicy Fruit gum. He could smell the smoke on her anyway.

When Frank opened the flat, rectangular present from his kids, he was perplexed to find a handsome silver cigarette holder with just two very skinny roll-ups inside. "But this isn't like tobacco, dad," FJ insisted. "Marijuana smells nice, it's pleasant."

"Are you telling me that all along you two are lawbreakers?" Frank asked. FJ and Juliet looked at each other conspiratorially. "Yes! Us and about half the country."

"Well, you can do what you damn please," said Catherine, sitting off to the side embroidering, her ankles primly tucked one behind the other, "but I'm not about to poison my lungs with filthy drugs at this late stage in my life." She broke into a cough and Frank kept staring down at the present, hiding his scowl. FJ longed to say something about her cigarette habit, but in this house no one spoke the truth out loud. There was plenty of chatter, mind you, just no candor.

Nope, here it was all smoke and mirrors. The outside world considered Frank to be a reliable guy and a bit of a jokester, famous for the time he put peanut butter in the holes of a rival's bowling ball. When he laughed with his buddies, he threw his head back and shook his last remaining strands of floppy hair back and forth. At home, though, he held his breath. No one knew Catherine like he did. To those outside the family, she radiated gregarious self-confidence. She had an affected way of talking that she was sure conveyed possession of the college degree she never got; and she moved with what she believed was an elegant formality, when really it was the result of a stiff waist-length bra and a constricting knee-long girdle. Her family feared her ragged edges, as did any salesgirl or waitress who crossed her. All the mirages of their lives belonged to Catherine – whether it was her smokes or the time Frank Junior had swallowed a bottle of aspirin when he was 15. To live with Catherine, you had to be able to figure out the forbidden topics and to leave the spin to her.

"Frank Junior has been under the weather," FJ heard Catherine telling his Aunt Emily the morning after he had his stomach pumped, "so I'm keeping him home from school for a couple of days." Catherine never even asked him what led to his attempt to kill himself. "Isn't life hard enough," she had said to Frank Senior at the dinner table, "without listening to the whines of a spoiled adolescent?"

As for lies, now that was a different story. If they added a gloss to life, if they painted her as more educated or wealthier than she was, then Catherine was all for lies -- not that she conceived of them as lies, exactly. For when they were sufficiently repeated or said with absolute conviction, lies turned for her from fabrication into elaboration, a mere literary flourish. She believed she was improving the world with her amplifications, making life more entertaining for those who came in contact with her.

FJ first comprehended that his mother inhabited an alternative world when he was about seven and he went with Catherine to the department store. It was one of the first times Catherine had driven into those new parking lots that you ascend by a spiral lane. She found the whole experience nerve-wracking and when she finally pulled the old 1953 Ford into a narrow parking slot, she scraped the passenger side of the car against a concrete divider. FJ remembered how he jumped a mile. “Ma! Watch it! You coulda killed me.”

Her hand had shot out, trying to slap him across the face, but hitting his ear instead. It was still ringing when they came out of the store.

Later, after dinner, Catherine sent him out to play. She and Frank put on the TV to watch a game and at the first commercial she said, “Oh darn, Frank. I forgot to tell you what happened when I was at Gimbels today. Someone must’ve hit the car while I was inside and they didn’t leave a note or anything. Scraped the whole side. You’re going to have a conniption when you see it.”

FJ happened to have come back into the house by the kitchen door to get a glass of water and heard what she said. “What?” he yelled, “but you hit the car on that wall, Ma.”

“You get in here young man.”

Frank Junior recognized that sharp tone in her voice: she was about to pretend. In that moment he grasped what a liar was. “You see what’s happening, Frank? He keeps fibbing. This child makes things up, just to hurt my feelings." She took on a stricken look. FJ didn't think his dad would fall for it, but Frank just turned back to watch the game.

Catherine had sneered then – it was a look he knew well from those terrible kids at school – and in front of his eyes his mother ceased to be a person he could depend on. It was, he would realize years later, the end of his childhood. "Get upstairs to your room young man. And forget playing outside after school. You're grounded until you stop your fibs."

Frank Junior hesitated for a few seconds, hoping in vain that his dad would look up. Then he dragged himself up to his bedroom. He was going to be her prisoner until he got big enough to escape.

"I don't even know how to smoke, for Christ's sake," Frank was saying to Frank Junior, starring into the silver container. "I wouldn't know what to do with the damned thing."

"We'll teach you, Frank," Juliet said in her soft, sweet voice, patting the old man's leg, the multiple beaded rings and bracelets like a graceful advertisement for her crafts shop. "I didn't know how to smoke cigarettes either, but I learned how to smoke joints."

"Joints?"

"Marijuana cigarettes. Like the ones in your lap."

"Why don't you both try it?" Juliet said, looking at Catherine, who sat ominously quiet in her corner. "We'll all smoke it together and it will be a fun evening. Something out of the ordinary. We wanted to find a really special way to celebrate Frank's 80th."

Frank Junior thought there was just enough hesitation to suggest that his parents were considering it, so he brought out his travel ashtray and a box of matches and held his hand out to Frank. "Give me the case, Dad, and I'll show you what to do."

Juliet got up and waved Catherine over. "Here, sit here, Catherine." Catherine winced at the use of her first name. How many times had she asked FJ to insist that Juliet call her Mother? So what if Frank didn't mind Juliet calling him Frank. She did not agree with this modern habit of using first names. FJ actually did raise it with Juliet, but she dismissed the idea "I don't have that 'mom' kind of feeling for her, honey. I'm sorry, I just don't, and I'm not prepared to fake it. There's too much faking in your family already."

Catherine stood up, but instead of joining them she went into the kitchen. "Count me out," she said over her shoulder. "And as for you Frank, do you really think Dr. Lombardi would approve?" She rattled around, doing up the last of the dishes and slamming a few things onto shelves before returning to the living room. "I'm going to bed now. Good night everyone. Drive safely, Frank Junior."

She pointedly said nothing to Juliet and mounted the steps with the air of an exhausted martyr.

So, the party was over. FJ put his travel ashtray back in his coat pocket and Juliet scooped the matches into her bag. “Happy birthday, Frank,” she said, bending over and kissing the single stripe of hair on top of his head.

Frank stood up and hugged his son and then let the two of them out of the door. The cigarette case remained on the coffee table where, next morning, Catherine found it and stowed it with the real silverware she claimed to have inherited from her mother, but which she had actually bought at a yard sale. She reasoned that the case fit in because it was silver. She never told Frank where it was. She couldn’t tell him because that night he died in his sleep.

There had never been a more bereaved widow than Catherine. She sobbed audibly right through the funeral service from behind the family curtain, wept lavishly at the cemetery, and lamented dramatically during visits from friends and neighbors. One evening the Shapiros from the house across the way came by with a casserole. Frank Junior flashed back to the time he had asked his mother about the blue numbers scribbled on Mr. and Mrs. Shapiro’s forearms. “Don’t keep bringing that up,” she had admonished him. “You weren’t even born. Why don’t we find something more pleasant to discuss?"

Mrs. Shapiro mumbled words of comfort, but Catherine cried, "You have no idea what I am going through! None whatsoever."

Oh how they had shared a passionate devotion and love for each other, she told each visitor. She neglected to mention that they hadn't had sex in about twenty years. Right around the time that Frank had two heart valves replaced, Catherine had been feeling pretty dry down there and when they had intercourse it was painful. The heart surgery had freaked Frank out, what with facing mortality and getting old. During his recovery he tried to make love to Catherine several times but she insisted that it was too dangerous for him. Naturally she didn't reveal the dryness and pain – that would be so inelegant. At her insistence, they had never had any discussion in which actual organs were named. "We don't," she liked to brag to her girlfriends, "say such things out loud."

In fact, although they had had a lot of it when they were younger, they had never talked about sex at all It was just one of the many topics she considered "not nice." So between his fears and her admonitions, Frank began having trouble getting erections. Not by his own hand, to be clear, but when he was with her. She barely touched him at all, afraid that he'd get the wrong message and think she was up for a frolic. Her repeated rejections literally deflated Frank. For two decades, when they were in company, they held hands and kissed and continued to play the romantic couple, but at night they lay apart on the bed as if surrounded by individual force fields.

Frank Junior was in his own state of shock after his dad's sudden passing. Not once, however, did Catherine ask him how he was doing or admit that he too was mourning. "You never really knew your father," she told FJ, with that sneer of hers, "You stopped living with us at 18. You never were all that involved with us."

He had adored his dad all these years, and always sustained a private relationship with him. "Don't forget," he answered his mother, "that we met for lunch at Antonio's at least twice a month for a beer and burger." When he saw the look on her face, he realized that Frank had never told her about their meetings.

"Don't be ridiculous," she answered. "You never did anything of the kind."

After several months of Catherine's unrelenting high-pitched mourning, FJ called in the doctor. "She's depressed," said the genius with the stethoscope. "Yes," FJ said, "and what can we do about it?" In her weakened state, Catherine complied with the doctor's directions to take a daily pill. She had never taken pills of any sort, let alone psychological medicines, considering them a sign of weakness. The crying stopped and she became wilted and benign. She discontinued her public displays of bereavement – at least the more histrionic gestures. She was satisfied with a single call per day from either FJ or Juliet. And then she found religion.

Not any particular religion – just the church down the street. The second Sunday she went to the church, an old man came down the aisle before the service began and asked to sit next to her.

"You may remember me as your husband Frank's old friend Victor. We were on the bowling league together many years ago. What a guy. I have been to your lovely home and I remember your pineapple upside-down cake."

Catherine was taken aback, confused, flattered. Luckily the service began and she didn't have to look at him, although she did sneak a peek while he sang one of the hymns with a lusty tin ear. He was unkempt, and his dry cracked lips and choppy haircut added nothing to the general impression. His hands, resting on the back of the pew in front of them, were blotchy and his shirtsleeves were grubby. In her eyes, though, he had two crucial things going for him: he was of the male persuasion and he wanted to step out with her.

She called Juliet and in a roundabout way mentioned that she had a new friend, Victor. "What kind of friend, Catherine?"

"A church friend. A religious man, a believer. Also a widower. He kissed my neck the first time he walked me home and I pushed him away."

When FJ came home that evening, Juliet said, "Your mother is being incoherent, but I think she is dating someone and I think it's sexual."

FJ called Catherine up right away. "I'm on my way over for a little visit, Ma, is there anything I can bring you?"

"A visit now?" She hesitated, raising red flags for FJ: Catherine's position had always been that she couldn't and didn't get enough of him.

"It's not entirely convenient," she added.

Now the red flags turned into an emergency siren. "See you soon," he said, putting down the phone and striding to his car. By the time he got there, he found his mother alone, although there were two dirty plates and two used coffee cups in the sink as well as a pineapple upside-down cake in the refrigerator with a sizable hunk cut out. Well! Catherine was back baking and entertaining. He tried questioning her, but FJ got very little information other than an admission that "a friend" had dropped by. She offered him no cake and seemed in a hurry for him to go.

Catherine's transformation from devastated, medicated widow to flirtatious, giddy lover was uncannily swift. It started with a cup of lemoned tea and Victor's impressed gratitude over the pineapple upside-down cake. This led her to invite him for dinner the following night. He turned up with empty hands, she was disappointed to see, but she had already decided – in contradiction to her lifelong belief – that elegant manners were not the be-all and end-all of civilization. In fact, she was never to receive a gift from him that she herself didn't pay for.

Victor was a "taker" and he was slovenly, there was no denying that, but he had chosen her. So many of her girlfriends had been widowed much longer than Catherine, but she was the one who had scored a man, even though she was in her 80s. At her age she wasn't going to earn an Olympic gold medal; she wasn't going to be an astronaut; she wasn't going to own a mansion. In her mind, finding a new man to step out with was the ultimate achievement.

And why take it slow? Were they kids with their whole lives in front of them? Victor was in a rush. They were aging adults. He felt a lust for her, he told her, and he didn't want to pretend otherwise. No one had ever spoken like that to her. Unbeknownst to her family, she had had several dates since Frank passed, and none of them had worked out. She felt she was being interviewed, like a nurse or a housekeeper. These men were looking for a caregiver, not a sweetheart. Victor was different and he was clear. "All those many years ago, Catherine, from the first time I got a look at you and tasted that cake, you sparked my interest. Of course out of respect for the holy bond of matrimony, I said nothing. But when I saw you so many years later in church, I felt that God had led you to me." She wrote a generous check to the church and decided it was her duty not to resist such a line.

Catherine continued to leave FJ and Juliet in the dark about her connection to Victor. "Do I ask you personal questions about your friends?" she responded when Juliet asked what was going on. They had no idea how quickly things were developing. Not, that is, until a couple of weeks later when FJ, having left work early one day, called Catherine to see if he could pick up any groceries for her before coming over to visit. Her voice mail clicked in. Just as it had when he had tried calling her during his lunch hour. He skipped the shops and went directly to her house. Although she didn't answer his knock, the curtains were open and he could see that the TV was on. He knocked harder, as he dug out her key from among the many on his chain.

He opened the door and called to her: "Ma? You home? Ma, where are you?" But he got no response. He checked all the downstairs rooms before heading up the stairs. From the landing he could see that the bathroom door was ajar and that the light was on. An odd smell wafted around and he could hear noise, too. Suddenly a woman shrieked. His heart sank and he ran in fear to push open the door.

His mother, buried in mounds of bubbles in her bathtub, surrounded by scented candles that were stinking up the room, looked up startled. As did the disheveled old man who sat facing her in the tub, holding up her foot and sucking on her big toe.

"Frank Junior! Shut that door and leave me in peace."

As he stood there frozen, he clocked the smoke tails of several sticks of incense and the big loofah sponge he had never seen before. Nor had he ever seen her naked back – rounded and marked with age spots and moles.

"Enough!" his mother said again.

He ripped his eyes from the bewildering scene in front of him and backed out of the bathroom, pulling the door shut behind him.

"Children," Catherine said to Victor. "Can't live with them. Can't live without them."

They laughed louder than the situation called for and then Victor reached behind him to dry his hands on a towel.

"One more puff?" he asked?

"After you, sir," she said, as he reached down to the ashtray on the floor. He put the lighter to the joint and inhaled. The night before, as she set the table for dinner, she'd decided to use her real silver. After all, what was she saving it for? The non-existent grandchildren? Who was a more important dining guest than Victor? There she discovered the silver cigarette holder the children had given to Frank Senior. She laid it next to Victor's dessert plate, and when he opened it he recognized the contents immediately.

"Shall we smoke some in the bathtub?" he had suggested.

"If you say so. I wouldn't know the first thing about it."

Now they lay in the water quietly, until Victor broke their silence.

"I think that FJ was simply worried about you. If he can't reach you on the phone – and remember, we decided not to answer it -- and then you can't hear him knocking because we're too busy being naughty up here, well then it's natural that he burst in on us!"

Catherine laughed. Victor continued, "If you had a computer and just sent him an email, then he wouldn't worry. And you wouldn't actually have to talk to him. And he could read it whenever he decided to. That's how the young people do it. It's very convenient, you know."

"Wouldn't know what to do with one."

"Oh that's not a problem. I'm an expert," Victor said. "Two, three lessons and you'll be a pro."

"Well, let me think about it. Meanwhile, the water's getting cold. Shall we get out?"

She stood up, full frontal, without any sign of the self-consciousness she had always felt, even as a young girl with a buxom shape. Victor wolf-whistled and ran his hand up her wet leg, grasping the inside of her thigh. "You're one hot tamale," he said for the umpteenth time. He stood up too and they climbed out of the tub gingerly, giving each other a hand. Victor grabbed a towel and rubbed her down, teasing her when he got to her rear crack and stopping to play with a nipple.

"Oh dear," Catherine giggled, "No one has dried me off since I was an infant."

"Their loss, Jane," he said. It was his nickname for her – after Jane Russell, the busty movie star of the 1940s and 50s. And it never failed to make her feel glamorous. She wondered if Victor had kept a pinup of Jane inside his locker during the war like the other G.I.s. She ran her fingers through her hair, lifting her chin and tilting her head in what she hoped look like a natural pose. While it might be thinning a bit, she was proud that her hair was still mostly brunette. She was the only girl in her circle who had never dyed her hair. She considered hair coloring very "common."

Victor finished rubbing her down and she realized that she was casually standing there, naked, as he toweled himself off. It just wasn't the sort of thing she had ever done before. Perhaps it was the comparison between herself and the shriveled Victor that gave her a sense of freedom. Perhaps it was his incessant lust and exaggerated compliments that gave her permission. But more likely it was her aroused sexuality. She felt she was making up for so many years without sexual satisfaction. That lubricant – what Victor called his "magic love juice" – had definitely changed things for the better. No problems with dryness anymore. Victor slathered his hand in lube, which allowed him to slide along the inner folds of her privates with a liberty neither she nor Frank had ever taken. It made her as slick and wet as a girl in her 20s.

But his hand was only part of the story. There were the vibrators too. Only in dirty jokes had she ever heard about sex toys and at first she was absolutely unwilling to let him approach her with that buzzing device. But after the first orgasm with it jammed against her clitoris – an organ for which she had no name, she was hooked.

Victor had developed his expertise out of necessity. Because of his medications, he couldn't get an erection, although he did have orgasms. Since he couldn't depend on his penis, he learned to use his mouth and his hands. He bought toys. He watched porn and got ideas. He had to work around erections and convince women to get him off in the ways they could. He became a sharpshooter when it came to the clitoris. He zeroed straight in to the most sensitive crevices. He figured the whole thing out. Once he had seen the power he gained from turning old women onto sex, seduction rivaled gambling as his favorite hobby. By the time he got to Catherine, he really knew his way around a woman's body.

His own love of sex was infectious and Catherine forgot to be embarrassed. He literally touched her where no one else had ever touched her. By simply assuming that she would, he got her to do things like lay naked on her back and throw open her legs to his lips.

But having never really had a free and unrepressed sex life before, Catherine confused the lustful satisfaction Victor gave her with a profound love. Victor became the most important person in her life, and she dated her devotion from that first time he had kissed the back of her neck. That one bold move had turned a depressed elderly widow into an aroused sex bomb.

The morning after Frank had walked in on Catherine, he grilled his mother over the phone, noting down every detail about Victor that he could extract from her. Afterwards, he called around to check him out and discovered that he had a reputation for seducing lonely women, getting them to buy him expensive presents and to bake him his favorite pastries, usually until he got caught with his next conquest. The people in the senior housing complex where he lived considered him a parasite with a tendency to spend too much of his girlfriends' money at the casinos. Apparently he always kept a couple of romances going at any one time, but no longer with folks in his own senior complex, where his sleazy reputation preceded him.

But when FJ tried to talk to Catherine about Victor, he was arrested by her vehemence. "That's just fine for you, Frank Junior, but this is the first time I've ever truly been in love and I'm going to pursue it whether or not you or your wife approves."

With that, nearly 60 years of marriage to his father were swept away as trifling. FJ was mortified for his father and shocked by how easily his mother was able to topple his own sense of personal history. If there was one thing he could have sworn was true, it was his parents' attachment. Why else would Frank Senior have stayed with her all those years?

That evening he got the first and last email his mother would ever send. "dear son and daughter-in-law this is my email address so please send photos love your mother Catherine."

"I can just hear Victor dictating to her," Juliet said.

"Or writing it for her altogether," FJ answered,

knowing Catherine's fastidious writing style, honed in florid, hand-written thank-you notes and sympathy cards.

The next time they visited Catherine, at her invitation, there was a desktop computer in a spacious corner of the dining room. It sat on a new computer table next to the all-color printer/fax/scanner/copier, and piles of photo and letter paper. The very fancy desk chair ("It'll be good for her back," Victor whispered to them) was bright red. Victor had taken Catherine and her credit card shopping.

In the following weeks, FJ and Juliet were overwhelmed by a deluge of group email blasts from Victor. Many were risqué in an offensive, old-fashioned way; others were undiluted right-wing polemics or racist cartoons; and every few days they received a smarmy personal email in 22 font capital letters updating them on Catherine's activities, her bowel movements (always an issue), and church news. They rarely heard from Catherine herself.

When Catherine got cancer, Victor immediately started pulling back. This was understandable, Catherine explained. His wife and daughter had both died of cancer and no one could blame him if he was reluctant to go through it yet again. But Catherine was not interested in anyone other than Victor taking care of her, besides the professionals like the visiting nurse and the home help that FJ arranged. She didn't want FJ and Juliet to come around in case Victor decided on one of his increasingly rare visits. Once the chemo reduced her hair to sparse tufts – in an ironic reminder of Frank Senior – she spent over $500 on a wig she never wore: it was put aside for the visits Victor failed to make.

After the first series of chemo, nothing had shifted, so the oncologist suggested that Catherine do another series with a different drug. After the second series failed too, the oncologist wanted to try a combination. "You're my toughest patient," she told Catherine, to great effect. "No one copes as well as you do." There was little that Catherine liked better than a compliment from an educated authority figure like a doctor. "I'm her toughest patient," she would boast to her friends, wishing she could have bragged a bit to the absent Victor.

FJ's contact at the complex where Victor lived heard that Victor was stepping out with a different woman from the same church, a widow with only one leg who had been left quite well off. He was seen driving her around in her late husband's luxury Oldsmobile, wearing the late husband's cashmere overcoat and fedora.

Catherine fought on, voluntarily subjecting herself to brutal medical treatments, motivated in the main to stretch out her time with Victor. Even pineapple upside-down cupcakes that she made for him failed to seduce him back. He didn't even return her calls. She was humbled by being dumped by this man of her dreams, but that feeling quickly turned to fury. Not at Victor ("It reminds him too much of his wife and child, poor man. It's hard to be so sensitive."), but at everyone else, not the least FJ – who was a living reminder of Frank, somehow now a villain in the background – and her daughter-in-law Juliet, who had never been quite right, if Catherine told the truth. It was one of those things that she and Frank Senior had never agreed on. He thought Juliet was just perfect, but Catherine knew otherwise. Juliet had a big mouth, said whatever she felt, and besides she served frozen foods to FJ. She wasn't ladylike and she wasn't much of a housekeeper. "But she's a kind, honest person," Frank would insist. "That's not good enough for *our* family," Catherine would reply.

FJ arranged for Meals on Wheels and a private caregiver several times a week. But then one day Catherine called him in tears. She had been constipated for five days, she said, and was beside herself from the pain. He drove right over to take her to the hospital, where she was admitted. After a day of testing, the doctors took FJ aside. "We're not sure why your mother is still being given chemo, just a couple of weeks at most before she is going to die. She should probably go into hospice."

FJ was in the unenviable position of disabusing

Catherine of the idea that she could win this thing by continuing to fight – something the oncologist had aggressively marketed to her – and of telling her that she had very little time left. "How dare you, Frank Junior," was her first reaction. "You just can't wait to put me in my grave. But my doctor said I was doing brilliantly. I'm only here for constipation."

When for the third time he came up against the same unyielding resistance to the truth, FJ brought in her hospital doctors to lay out her terminal situation to her. Her cancer had metastasized. It had spread to her liver, her spine, her lungs. Time was short. The team of residents might look like a gaggle of college students, but the Dr. before their names was authority enough for Catherine. "We feel hospice is the best solution."

Catherine shook her head no, but when the day passed and there was no sign of Victor, she gave up and agreed to be transferred to the hospice.

As they waited for the ambulance to transport her, Catherine spoke in a weak voice to FJ. "Frank, bring me my bag." He handed her the faux leather purse and she dug around in it until she came up with his father's Rolex, the retirement gift he had received with such pride from his company. "I want you to have this, son. I was hoping to give it to Victor, but it looks like I won't have a chance to. He once told me he would never step foot in another hospice. So instead of it going to waste, here, you take it."

FJ didn't know what to do. He didn't even want to touch the now-tainted gold. Her arm sank down to the bed and the watch rolled into the folds of the thin hospital blanket. It was the last conversation they were ever to have. It was no comfort to him that she had, as he would later say in her eulogy, maintained her personality to the end.

Anna Lynne Kneels

Franklin

Anna Lynne was in her early 40s when she decided that she had simply had enough of her husband Franklin.

She had met him when she was a virginal 20, in the midst of a short, uncharacteristic period of mild cynicism. Franklin became the focus of her rather muted revolt against her wealthy family's habitual fine taste. Handsome in a muscular way, Franklin alternated between brash and sullen, but she found his unpredictability exciting. She wasn't aware of his drinking. Her parents were calm and patient, trusting that she'd soon get over this stage.

However, by 22, Anna Lynne was married and pregnant – in that order. By 33 she had two daughters and two sons and a growing sense that being with Franklin was a waste of her time. Every morning at breakfast, she and the kids crowded around one end of the table chattering. Across from them, Franklin hid behind his newspaper grunting at the sports pages. She felt she was starting each day with a hot steaming cup of regret.

Sometimes when things deteriorate in a relationship, you reach that point when you can't bear the other person's innocent personal habits –

their way of dusting off their shoulders or of shaking the dog's leash before hanging it up. You find yourself so filled with distaste that you begin to dislike yourself for being so petty. Anna Lynne had moved into that stage. She wished she didn't cringe at the sound Franklin made when he Q-tipped his ears every morning – a kind of clearing of his throat as if he were penetrating so deeply in his ear that it was tickling his tonsils. And his bathrobe – he still hadn't decided whether to tie it above or below his not inconsiderable beer belly. She understood that she wasn't being fair – he'd been doing that Q-tip thing forever, after all – but her reaction was involuntary.

Anna Lynne failed to share Franklin's own sense of himself. He felt that he was a practical man; she felt he lacked wit and imagination. She understood – because he told her so often – that by building their family's lives around her own community, she had turned him into an outsider in his own home. Technically, it was her house – or rather one of her family's properties, but neither of them ever mentioned that. Nor did he ever admit to seething anger over the lack of even a single comfortable chair in the house among all the antiques. The absence of a bit of plush upholstery, he explained to her, was one of the main reasons he hung out in the man-cave he had fashioned for himself in the basement. This rationalization, while only a tiny part of the truth, worked for both of them.

When he lost the job her uncle had arranged for him – one in a long line of family employments that had dribbled out of his unambitious hands – Franklin suggested that they both live off her income. True, her family owned a number of substantial rental properties, four local car dealerships, and an executive jet dealership; and true, she had a regular generous income from her grandfather's estate; but she was offended by his refusal to even try to earn a living.

Franklin knew that, on paper, he was lucky to have Anna Lynne. Beautiful, wealthy, a good mother, baked a mean berry pie – but as far as he was concerned, Anna Lynne's attitude sucked. She looked down on him and it made him want to hide in the basement or in his local bar with a fat cigar for the day. "You have a grandiose work ethic – as long as someone else is doing the work," he would have said if only they'd had the habit of speaking the truth to each other.

When he first met her, Franklin had been dazzled. To him, she was special, different. He would never forget the first time he pulled two pins out of the complicated bun she always wore and her light brown hair cascaded down to the center of her back. He wondered what other delights were hidden behind her composed exterior. There was something so soft, clear-spoken, and peaceful about Anna Lynne – and it took Franklin years of maturing to realize that there were lots of people like her; they just didn't circulate in his old neighborhood.

What had seemed like delicacy to him at first, now stank of fastidiousness. Her unique calm he now attributed to the fact that she had never had to work a day in her life, never had to worry about bills.

He had hardly touched her before they were married. Their honeymoon was pretty hot – he came just about every time he got near her – but it was downhill from there. Until he had hooked up with Anna Lynne, most of his sexual experience with a woman had involved either a payment to a pro or a lot of alcohol. Most of the time, now, excitement was a matter between his own hand and mind.

Anna Lynne didn't drink and didn't like him to make love to her when he was drinking – which he did increasingly. Sober wasn't really his natural state. Although Franklin and Anna Lynne had managed to create four kids together, neither of them had had much fun doing it.

As the chill settled over their marriage, Franklin reverted to his bachelor behavior. Once the kids were off to school – the driver took them even though Franklin had offered many times – and Anna Lynne had gone to her charity meetings or museum luncheons, he went into his man cave, watched some pornography, and passed an hour or two in leisurely masturbation. It was the one area of the house and the one endeavor that he could call his own. No one, especially not the squeamish Anna Lynne, could touch him as well as he touched himself.

Sometimes Anna Lynne returned home while he was still in the basement, but she never came down to knock on the door of his man-cave. She suspected that he was up to something down there, but she found his isolation convenient. If he went upstairs when he heard her come in, their small talk was repetitive and boring. She never pried. She wasn't interested. So for the last year or two, when she returned home, he slipped out the garage door and headed to the bar.

One day, when Franklin was watching a video that would have bewildered Anna Lynne altogether, he felt stabbing pains in his thumb joint. He shook his hand and then returned to playing with himself, but the pains persisted. He rested his hand until the next day, when he again found it difficult to stroke himself. He went upstairs for an ice pack, but that only gave him temporary relief.

His doctor sent him to a physical therapist who used electro-stimulation and manipulation, but it only relieved the pain until he got back to his basement retreat and tried to use the hand. Arthritis, the doctor declared at their follow-up appointment, and prescribed pain pills. The news that it was a chronic, not a temporary condition put Franklin into a bit of a tailspin. How was he going to pass his days?

He began to invest in too much beer and too many boxes of cigars to pass around to his friends in the old neighborhood bar he returned to. At least there his buddies were happy to see him, and to relieve him of his spare change around the pool table. They admired his escape uptown, without any idea of what his life was actually like. He renewed a friendship with a former high-school girlfriend who had an apartment around the corner from the bar, where they spent many hours in a shared alcoholic haze.

One day he stumbled home and found Anna Lynne, her hands folded neatly in her lap as she sat at the edge of the nineteenth century love seat, surrounded by her lawyer, her accountant, and her rich uncle. Franklin's bags were packed and were standing neatly in the vestibule and a sheaf of papers filled the handsome leather case the lawyer put in his hand. "Read them at your convenience," the lawyer said, "I think you'll find everything in order."

Anna Lynne and her uncle had pulled this all together in a week. The idea had been born at a long lunch Anna Lynne had spent with her close friend Doreen.

"How is it going with Franklin?" Doreen had asked. "You never mention him at all anymore."

"We live different lives," she answered, with a candor she shared only with Doreen. "He's down in his room in the basement playing dirty videos, and the kids and I are upstairs living our regular lives."

"Do you still have sex together?"

Anna Lynne looked at her friend, shaking her head with a frown. "Of course not. We haven't in quite some time."

"Then why drag it out? Why don't you end it?"

Anna Lynne had never considered divorce. It simply had never entered her mind. But once Doreen gave voice to the idea, it was immediately clear to Anna Lynne that she would talk to her uncle that very day to get things moving.

Meanwhile, Franklin, stunned, looked from the briefcase to his wife. Anna Lynne said nothing, just nodded and smiled with what seemed like a sense of relief. She glanced at her uncle, who then spoke up. "I've set you up in a furnished one-bedroom in one of my buildings, Franklin, and you can stay there for a year. That should give you time to get on your feet."

Franklin turned from the lawyer back to Anna Lynne, but she didn't meet his gaze. He couldn't take it in. What was happening? Were they actually throwing him out? But he was her husband. He was legal.

“Shall we have Lou help you out with your bags?” asked the accountant. And without waiting for an answer, he opened the door and waved to the gardener positioned near the front bushes.

Franklin’s life had changed without warning and with a swift efficacy only the wealthy could pull off. Anna Lynne wore a muted expression of reprieve.

“What about the kids?” Franklin asked her, rubbing his thumb unconsciously.

“We’ll work out the details very soon,” the lawyer answered.

Franklin followed his final bag out to his car, suddenly looking two sizes too small for his clothes. His head dropped onto his chest; his chest sank. Talking silently to himself, he never looked back. He would be dead – of resentment, of sexual frustration, and of alcohol poisoning – before the year of free rent ran out.

John

It had been decades since Anna Lynne’s late husband had been escorted out of her home by her lawyers. Her four grown children were now all settled elsewhere – one in London and the rest in nearby states. Her inherited wealth and beauty cushioned her life; avid interests filled it. She was as aware of her privilege as she was of her deprivation: her love of literature and the visual arts highlighted how little she knew of stirring sex or romantic drama. Franklin had been a silly mistake, although she was grateful to him for their children, who were a constant support to her. He had died shortly after the divorce was finalized, leaving her memories of him frozen in a period of distasteful incompatibility. She was relieved to find herself single and free, not the least after the children had grown up and left the house.

Her girlfriends convinced her to try dating, so during her 50s and early 60s she went out briefly with a number of forgettable men. Some of them were such "gentlemen" that she took their prudence for disinterest. Other made bumbling attempts to grope her, reminding her of the unpleasant touches of her awkward ex-husband. When reading a powerful romance or viewing a painting depicting a charged embrace, she recognized that her sexual experiences with Franklin, the only man with whom she had ever been fully intimate, didn't really compare. But she was grateful that her life was rich nonetheless.

Then she met John.

She was 69 and he was 77. He had been widowed eight years earlier. Tall, tweedy and relaxed, he was also tough in unexpected ways. John's grip was so strong and intense that the first time he closed his fingers around her upper arms to pull her up for a kiss, Anna Lynne was startled by her own elevated level of anticipation.

"What's wrong?" he asked with a soft smile when she resisted slightly.

"I don't know. Your grasp …" She couldn't explain.

"Shall we try again?" He looked at her with an absolute confidence that made her lower her eyes. He wrapped his hands around her upper arms once more and she strained backwards, away from him -- not, she soon realized, because she wanted to get away, but because she wanted him to compel her to come closer.

And he did. He pulled her into his chest and she felt that she was surrounded by him. It wasn't just his height or the width of his shoulders on his slender frame. It was his attitude. And then he did something completely unexpected. He grabbed a handful of her expensively coiffed hair and pulled her head back. As he looked in her eyes calmly, he lifted her chin with his other hand and kissed her. It was like no other kiss she had ever experienced. No, this kiss possessed her mouth – or rather, it possessed her being.

When he released her hair and chin, she thought she would swoon, but he took her hand and led her to the couch where he made love to her with an almost scary fervor, but without taking off any of their clothes. It was chaste in that sense, she thought after he left, but fiery. Nearly 70, and she went through the rest of the night wet and aroused.

At her urging, he was back the next evening and their clothes came off very rapidly. He introduced her to reckless passion. All he needed from her was ecstatic submission. For weeks they fell on each other with surprising rapture, but he did not penetrate her – not with his fingers and not with his penis. Not for several months. It wasn't about intercourse – it was about heightened sensations she had never imagined, derived from his kaleidoscopic erotic imagination.

Daydreaming on her balcony about John one day, she realized that there was in fact penetration. He had a way of jamming his finger into her mouth, of rooting around with it under her lips on her gums and then of pushing it down her throat too far. She'd gag and ask, "Why?" He'd smile and answer, "Practice."

After a couple of months, during a standing hug, he grabbed both of her ears and pulled down so firmly that she sank to her knees to avoid the pain. He unbuckled his belt and whipped it out of his slacks. Before she realized what he was doing, he had unzipped his fly and pulled out his cock. He bent his knees to cup her chin with his other hand.

"Open," he said with a smile.

When she didn't respond immediately, he squeezed her nostrils closed so that she had to open her mouth to breathe. He then stuffed his cock, still soft, into her mouth, pulling her face against the coarse hair of his crotch.

“Look up at me,” he said. “Now,” he insisted when she didn’t.

She looked up but her eyes were closed. He dropped her hair and stroked her face with such a soft and loving touch that she opened her eyes, connecting with his. At that moment, she felt him swell so suddenly that she pulled away, choking.

Pleased, he helped her to her feet and then led her to the bedroom. This kind of scenario would be repeated in many versions as their relationship became a roller coaster of excitement, from power to compliance to explosion.

John became her private miracle. The two of them isolated themselves in her bedroom, settling into a pattern of getting together on Wednesdays and weekends. In between there were emails and phone calls, often including debriefing sessions about recent bedroom encounters and plans for their next adventures.

After a few months, affection grew like a vine around the core of their physical attraction, and Anna Lynne and John started spending some of their Wednesdays and weekends going out. As soon as they realized that theirs was going to be an ongoing connection, they went public. John’s son was far away and didn’t have a particular point of view, but John’s friends approved of her. Anna

Lynne's kids were wary, but accepting, especially when she reassured them that she had no intention of making an honest man out of John.

Even now that everyone close to them knew about the affair, they kept to their Wednesday/weekend schedule.

"Are you going to live together?" her best friend Doreen asked. Doreen, short and slender, was from a similar background to Anna Lynne's – her father had owned several mines in Zimbabwe until liberation when he fled with a lot of money to the States.

"By no means," Anna Lynne answered. "You know me. I have to have time to talk to my girlfriends on the phone and to sit on the balcony and brood. The only man I lived with was Franklin, and I am still amazed that it lasted so long. Anyway, I haven't shared my space since my kids moved out. I don't want to change my life for anyone. If he were to move in, it would turn our sparkling affair to dull. John's like some very sweet cream in my coffee; if I had to pick up his socks or worry about his diet, it would be, well, like switching to stale water."

One Wednesday evening John didn't turn up at 7:00 as usual. Anna Lynne waited until 7:30 to call him. When he answered the phone, she could hear a lot of noise. "Hold on," he said, "Let me turn down the news."

"Where are you, sweetheart?"

"Stretched out in my recliner in front of the TV. And you, baby?"

"I'm waiting for you."

There was silence. More silence.

"Is it Wednesday?" John's voice was tight.

"It is."

More silence.

"I'll shower and be there within the hour."

She chalked it up to absent-mindedness, perhaps a senior moment, as by now John was 81. When he arrived, he was distracted and they did not even make love.

In the morning he told her, "Something's not right, Anna Lynne. "

And then he told her about some incidents he had not mentioned before. He had left his wallet on the counter at the pharmacy; but when the next customer had called out to him, waving it, John hadn't recognized it as his own. Another day he had parked his full grocery cart next to his car, opened the driver's door and driven away. Words were elusive, names were blanked out, and suddenly he felt like he had two left feet.

Once John confessed these incidents to Anna Lynne, they both became vigilant. His situation changed rapidly and within a few months he was riddled by anxiety. She found it exhausting to have to talk him down so often, as every lapse of memory made him fret.

One time she just sat in her living room for a couple of minutes and watched him flap his arms and shake his head as he pressed, as if against a strong wind, from one room to the other, muttering, "The keys are gone. The keys are gone."

"Let me help you," Anna Lynne sighed, putting down her book and going over to him. But during these episodes, it was tough for her to penetrate his distress. Sometimes he didn't notice her at all, he'd be so deeply wrapped up in his search. Her pleasure, her ecstasy used to be the object of his intense concentration. Now he was laser-focused on his failing abilities.

She went to the table in the front hallway and there, in the ceramic dish, were John's keys – just where he always put them. "They're here, honey," she called to his shuddering retreating back. It took him several more frantic steps until he came to a halt, turned back to her and spotted the keys. His neck lengthened, his shoulders relaxed, his hands stopped their flapping and the real John ebbed back in.

His son flew in and took him to the doctor's to get the results of the tests he had been given ten days earlier. He had dementia, probably due to Alzheimer's. It took John just a few hours to swallow that information. His son sat in John's living room dumbstruck, while John paced in front of him. “Let’s look this all up,” his son said, going to the computer to Google “dementia.”

He read from the screen, tossing out facts and figures at John, who continued to stride from room to room. In the middle of some medical explanation, John interrupted. “I need to sell the house and settle in wherever it will be that I’m going to be looked after.”

“What about Anna Lynne? Can’t she take care of you?”

John shook his head. “That’s not an option. Not for me, it isn’t. That isn’t what we’re about.”

His son did something he had never done before, even when his own children were born: he took off two weeks from work. John called Anna Lynne to tell her that he and his son needed to make certain arrangements and that once everything was sorted, he would come back to her. She didn’t hear from him again for over two weeks. Her body ached for his dominating grip and her mind longed to fly off to that state of excitation that replaced all thoughts and worries.

John and his son identified a facility with levels of care – from independence to a locked Alzheimer unit. They found a realtor who put John’s large house on the market, a lawyer who processed all the medical and power-of-attorney paperwork, and an estate planner to simplify his finances.

Finally his son returned to his own home and

John came to spend the weekend with Anna Lynne. "Why," she objected as he filled her in, "must they name the place Pond View? It seems like every place they build as an elder warehouse has some trite landscapey name."

John's house sold quickly, despite the weak market, and Anna Lynne found herself sucked into the vortex of a downsizing not her own. To pack John's boxes she had to miss a poetry reading she had helped organize. The work itself bothered her elbow tendinitis. A few days later she was determined to make her board meeting at the museum, but instead succumbed to John's depression and need.

The schedule they had always kept began bleeding out of the bedroom and all over their calendars. Wednesday became Tuesday-Wednesday-Thursday, full of errands and medical tests. Weekends became clogged with crates and bubble wrap.

Anna Lynne fought to dissipate the hovering cloud of despair and insisted that they get naked. She wanted John to remember what it was that had brought them together. Without sex, their relationship lost its core. From the start, they had been all about pleasure.

"You didn't sign up for this, Anna Lynne," John said one night with uncharacteristic candor. He was aware that she had even taken over their lovemaking, stroking his body, squeezing his shaft, and trying to seduce back the powerful lover she had fallen for.

"No, I didn't. I'll do what I can," she said, remembering her complaints to Doreen that morning about John's increasing dependence on her now that he had given up driving. "Clinginess," she had said to her friend, "just doesn't have sex appeal. My own life is evaporating. My daughter wants me to visit her and her twins in London, and my son keeps putting his kids on the phone to tell me how much they'd like to see Nana in Philadelphia. But John gets desperate when I mention traveling."

Laying her own hand on Anna Lynne's, Doreen took a deep breath before speaking. "John has dementia. You don't. If you don't visit your kids now, when exactly do you plan on doing it?" John's rapid decline had been the catalyst for several conversations between Doreen and Anna Lynne about their own mortality. "It might be trite, but it sure is right," Doreen said in a singsong tone, "Life is short." Anna Lynne squeezed her dearest friend's hand in gratitude.

Anna Lynne spent the next couple of weeks interviewing people to take care of John, not just because she wanted to go away, but because it was time. Then she went to London for eight weeks to visit her daughter and grandchildren.

On her return, she had a message to call John's

son. “Dad was moved to the locked unit,” he told her. “First he became disoriented and uncooperative. Then he started, well, um, stroking himself in public all the time – in the dining room, during bingo. The doctor told me that this is a known symptom of the disease for some people. I feel for the poor man.”

She drove to Pond View and was pointed towards his new accommodations. She was buzzed into the unit and as she walked into the common room she saw John, standing in front of a large mirror, tugging at the crotch of his pants. He was wearing what looked to be simple medical trousers, just blue material drawn in at the waist.

John looked very perplexed and disturbed and then Anna Lynne realized why. The pants had been put on him backwards and the drawstring was knotted behind his back. He was unable to open them by himself, especially in his confusion. She felt herself choking up as she recalled the slick way in which he used to open the buckle of his belt and slide it free of his pants – half menacing and half teasing her. She teared up as she flashed back to how he would undo his button and then lower his zipper inch by inch, nodding downward to her in a shortcut command that would bring her to her knees.

Did he still share those memories? Anna Lynne came up beside John and made eye contact in the mirror. He didn't seem to recognize her; but when he turned to face her, she responded to her own charged recollection of his signals and sank down, her face at crotch height, her eyes seeking his. For a moment she believed that he remembered, until he turned right back to the mirror to yank at his pants.

A nursing aide came over to Anna Lynne and silently offered her a hand. Anna Lynne took it gratefully and struggled to pull herself back up. She smoothed her hair unconsciously although nothing had disturbed it. As dramatic as the experience had been for her, no one other than the aide seemed to have noticed at all. She stood still, alone, conscious of being immaculately dressed in this unit of backward pajamas and chair restraints, and acutely aware that this would be her last sexual encounter with John. The situation which had metaphorically brought him to his knees had literally exiled Anna Lynne from hers.

Who's Leading This Dance, Anyway?

I don't even believe in marriage, but a person's got to make a living, doesn't she, and if people *will* persist in taking a matrimonial path, well, if I don't profit from the error of their ways, some other dance teacher will. Back in the 40s and 50s I taught dance at the lovely Goldberg Ballroom that was downtown at the corner of Smith Ave. and Linfield St. Then it was large groups of people brushing up their foxtrot and swing during the week so they'd be ready for the popular weekend dances. I had more energy than I knew what to do with, so I forged a career out of my best talent.

And the weekend dances weren't just dances. They were dinner and entertainment, too. Mannie Goldberg was the MC – his dad had built the place. They'd have a comedian and they'd have a singer and then my dance partner Louie and I would perform, too. Sometimes we'd do a samba – Louie loved the costumes for that one – and sometimes we'd do the jitterbug. It was like going to the Catskills without having to get in your car.

Louie and I won so many trophies that when I moved into this senior housing complex I had to box them up and put them in storage, because they sure could not fit into a one-bedroom apartment. I miss Louie, but it is nice to hear from his lifelong roommate Sam now and again, although Sam was never much of a dancer. Not that he ever skipped even a single one of our performances, except when he had to go to a work conference. He was a kitchen designer and he traveled to Home Shows. I was always sorry when that happened because then Louie's dancing wouldn't be as inspired as usual.

Still, I gotta bless Louie and I gotta bless my feet for feeding me all these years. I have always liked being my own woman, but most people thought it was my bad luck to be single. Everyone, even Louie, pushed me to step out with this man or that man – but I knew better. I didn't want no one telling me what to do and when to do it. I saw enough of that in my own house where my mother didn't have a moment's peace and quiet, what with my father bossing her around all the time. She was stuck with a mean, ungrateful man who never spoke a word of praise to her, or to me for that matter. Stuck till the day she gave up and died.

I didn't want to be stuck. I wanted to be free. No man was going to leave me free once I wore his ring, so I just wore my own rings. They weren't gold and they weren't diamonds, but they were mine. And they did not obligate me.

By the early 60s the Goldberg Ballroom wasn't drawing the crowds like in the old days. The kids weren't interested and the place had become pretty run-down. Seedy, even. They laid off all their dance teachers except me. Well, they laid me off too, but they'd call me in for sessions instead of keeping me on payroll. They gave the place a coat of paint and started hosting weddings instead of dances. That's where I started giving private lessons for couples before the big day, creating simple show-off type dances for them to do at their reception.

When the Goldberg Ballroom was torn down and one of those new high-rise parking lots was built in its place, I was left to fend for myself. I swallowed my pride and taught at an Arthur Murray school, and that was humiliating. For a while I even managed the place, but their methods were so shoddy and their teachers so incompetent that I felt dirty day in and day out.

Finally I started doing the rounds of the senior centers, getting those old people back up on their feet. I did that until I ended up in one of those places myself. Luckily my living room has a wooden floor because I'm not fully retired, or anything like that. I keep myself listed on a local dance website offering private lessons. And my neighbors recommend me to their grandchildren. Calls of interest dribble in, not the least from frustrated white engineers with Latin girlfriends who go out dancing without them, but that's another story. I also hear from engaged couples preparing for their weddings who have remembered at the last minute that they are supposed to open up the first dance once the music begins.

So I get a call from some Ruthie, great-niece of a neighbor, who wants to surprise her fiancé with a couple of dance lessons before their upcoming wedding. She has, keeping with tradition, waited until less than a month before their due date to look for a teacher. I suggest that two lessons won't be all that optimal. "Let's look at our datebooks and see if we can fit in six sessions," I say. "That way we can make a big splash with this thing on your – your special day."

I almost choke on that "special day" phrase – it's all part of my marketing, as they say nowadays.

I'm not a fan of piling on the sweet talk, but a person's got to make a living. Having never entered the marital game myself, I've sat back and watched generation after generation volunteering for this particular kind of prison. Oh the hours I've wasted listening to my girlfriends claim to be jealous of my freedom because Moshe did this to them or Irving did that. I grant them their pride in their kids – at least the ones who aren't still at home at 50 because of the schizophrenia or the divorce. Grandchildren are wonderful too, but then I think of how much money I've saved on bar mitzvah and birthday gifts by avoiding marriage. In fact, I always say that I would've ended up in the poor house if I had ever wanted liquor, furs, or offspring.

Overall, this marriage game has more minus than plus from what I have observed over 82 years. However, what can I tell you? There's nothing like $60 per hour to damp down the scruples, so when Ruthie gives her guy Lawrence his surprise and he agrees to come along, we make a first appointment. I warn them to bring their datebooks and also soft shoes in consideration of the poor downstairs neighbors.

"Hi," Ruthie says at my door, huffing a bit from her decision to take the stairs instead of the elevator to the fourth floor. She thrusts out one sweaty hand while she tugs on the under-wire of her bra with the other. She should try those steps at my age. I reach up to shake her hand – she is a tall girl, and then I notice Lawrence huddling behind her, his smile hobbled by a missing incisor and his height no match for hers. "Yes," he says with his uneven smile, reaching out to shake my hand next. "Yes," he repeats at least one or two more times, nodding and smiling with his gums and gap displayed. What's with this guy, I wonder. Is he miserable or just awkward, because he sure is something. Is he always like this or is he scared of dancing?

By the time I turn around, Ruthie has already taken herself inside, thank you very much, and Lawrence and I follow her. She is on my couch taking off her grown-up pumps with heels and putting on her sneakers. She pats the couch next to her, bangs on it really – oy! what a dust cloud she raises – and Lawrence, nodding rapidly, covers my tiny living room in three hasty strides to sit his tush down where she is pointing.

Before I can open my mouth, she adjusts her bra and says, "Now here's my idea. I'd like to do a samba at the wedding. My uncle by marriage is Puerto Rican which means that I've got Latin fire in my blood." Lawrence murmurs in support, all his teeth but the phantom one exposed, and she pats his thigh without looking at him. "I've brought my favorite samba songs," she says, digging a CD out of her bag and handing it to me. *Salsa Through the Ages*, the flea market compilation says.

I take it with me as I cross the room and sit on my comfy chair. Have I ever seen one person make more blunders in just a couple of sentences? Probably. I take a deep breath. I know perfectly well that lots of non-dancers confuse samba and salsa. Not all of them, though, do it with so much confidence. So she's never heard of Brazil: it's not a crime. Keep to the point, I remind myself. Don't make fun of the customers.

"Let me give you a little outline of what I offer," I begin, "Trust me, it has worked beautiful every time. I've made a thousand weddings sparkle." That's my catch-phrase: Make Your Wedding Dance Sparkle. A friend's son got me 300 business cards made up for just $15 with my name and phone number and that phrase. I still have about 280 of them. I should put them in storage with my trophies.

Anyway, I give them my song and dance, as it were. I can teach them to perform a scrumptious Latin routine to surprise and entertain their guests. I've done this for so many happy couples and they have all told me afterwards that it was the high point of their day. It puts the spotlight where it belongs: on the happy couple. All the guests are seated and then out comes the couple to perform at a professional level and no one even knew they could dance.

They glance at each other and Ruthie raises her eyebrows as if to say, The old bag has something here. Lawrence nods.

Then I tell them that surprise is the key to success. "Don't," I say, looking from Ruthie to Lawrence, "tell anyone. Only just your video-taker and your photographer. Don't even tell your parents that you're taking dance lessons. Trust me, on the day they'll faint from pride. You'll have your MC say this announcement right before he puts on your performance music." I hand them a printed page that says: "To our dear guests. We have planned this dance as a surprise present to all of you to thank you for your love and support and for coming to our wedding. Because you are here, we will never forget our happiness. So here is our gift to you."

When they finish reading, they look up at me. “Oh,” Ruthie says. Lawrence watches to see how she’ll respond. “I imagined doing the usual thing – the happy couple comes out on the floor to start the dance and then the parents join in and then the friends….” Her voice trails off as an image of herself and her groom alone as headliners in the middle of the ballroom takes form in her imagination.

“This is different,” I add. “Take advantage of having a professional teacher, why don’t you. I can choreograph a unique routine just for you. You’ll be the center of attention. Your guests will be amazed, especially if you keep the plan quiet, because they’ll be expecting the same old same old. You have your moment and then you can invite everyone else on to the dance floor.”

Ruthie is starting to picture the staging, the attention, the triumph – and soon she and Lawrence are nodding in near unison. “Good, then,” I say, putting her tacky CD out of sight, “Let’s start. Stand up.”

Ruthie pops up, adjusting her bra yet again and then her ruffled blouse and then her flowery skirt. She’s not making a great impression on me. She’s like a pushy saleswoman with total confidence in what she’s peddling, who fails to convince anyone to trust her. She’s a bit slimy or as Louie used to say, oily. Meanwhile Lawrence stands in one smooth and easy movement. I bet you an apple strudel that he'll be a much better dancer than her.

"We'll dance the meringue because it's the dance with the easiest footwork. It's like walking – just One, two, One, two." I show them, my hips shifting with the rhythm, as I make a little circle in my tiny living room.

"And now we'll do it together." I place them side-by-side behind me, so that they can watch my hips. "Try to imitate me, okay? Step on to the balls of your feet, hold up your elbows parallel to the ground, and step in place. Aaaand...," I draw out the word so they will realize we are starting, "One, two, One, two."

Once they have grasped the basic step, I put on some slow meringue music and lead them, still side-by-side, forward for eight counts, back for eight, and in place for eight, repeating until the end of the tune. Their breathing becomes just a little bit labored from the effort.

Now, though, it is crunch time. "Have a drink and sit down again," I tell them, waving toward the pitcher of ice-water and the glasses on the table next to the couch. In the early days, I used to give my students cold Tang, but that patriotic drink seems to have gone out of favor. "We need to discuss leading and following."

Here's the problem. I have certain views of leading and following and they are not what you would call orthodox. Many professionals object to my views, but I still hold them. I developed these ideas when I was dancing with Louie. The Goldbergs had given us the keys to the Ballroom and it was like our private studio. For besides rehearsing for the shows, we would dance for our own pleasure. And I would lead and Louie would follow. This was a secret between us. I didn't see any reason for us not to be public about it, but he wouldn't hear of it.

And what a follower Louie was. He could elongate his neck and tilt back his head during the waltz like nobody else. If we danced the rhumba, he was more seductive than the Queen of Sheba, with his little hips swishing back and forth. Dance worked wonders for Louie. If you saw him walking down the street, well he wasn't all that dazzling, just a schlump with glasses. But when I took him in my arms and he could follow like he was meant to do, well that was something else. He became beautiful. He glowed like a glitterball. He made me laugh with the joy of our partnership. When we rehearsed alone, that was the only time we were truly ourselves.

I much preferred to lead. I liked to be able to choreograph the dance, to control the routine, and to interpret the music. As a follower you couldn't do all that. Your job was to float and twirl. I was never much for floating. Leading suited me much better, although I didn't ever get to do much of it except behind closed doors with Louie – and with private students who were learning to follow.

Even though Louie was so reluctant to switch in public, after he died I decided that it wasn't such a big crime and that I was going to give my students the option. Why not? Would the sky fall if a woman led a man? Would the Cossacks turn up in the lobby? No, it was really not a crime against nature to let people choose what they would rather do – as long as they did it well.

So I've been giving my students this choice – even though people rarely take advantage of it. I tell this couple what I tell every new student, "Leading and following are the fundamentals of ballroom dancing – whether it's the waltz, the swing, or the cha-cha. But who should be a leader and who should be a follower?"

I stop for a second, see if they are understanding me. Lawrence is nodding his head, but he seems to do a lot of that. She's looking at me, suspicious-like. I go on. "It used to be decided by whether you were a man or a woman. But it doesn't have to be like that. It really should depend on what kind of person you are and how you suit the role."

Oh dear. Ruthie is knitting her eyebrows, unsure where I'm taking this. Lawrence has relaxed his face for the first time. I think I'm making him feel hopeful. I notice Ruthie towers over him when they are sitting – her torso must be extra long and her legs very short. He must be the opposite. For a second I wonder what she's going to think when she sees the photos of her sitting next to Lawrence at the wedding party reception table.

I rush to finish. "Let's talk about the difference between these two roles. A leader choreographs the dance. That is to say, leaders think ahead and plan for the next steps. Leaders are responsible for health and safety. That means they've got to be aware of the whole room so as to avoid running into other couples or spinning their partners out picture windows. Leaders need musicality: that's the professional term for having a good ear, knowing when to start a dance step and how to interpret the music. Most of all, leaders have to learn leader-language and communicate to their follower what to do."

It's been a long speech. Even so, I keep going. "To sum it up, the main job of the leader is to make the follower look fabulous. Anything that gets in the way of that is the leader's fault. So can either of you tell me why it's worth all the hard work to lead?"

Ruthie and Lawrence look at each other and then back at me. "To be in control!" I say.

Ruthie doesn't know what to think, so she asks the obvious. "And followers?"

"Good following is all about surrendering to the leader. Followers do as they are told, in the rhythm of their leaders. They have to be yielding, to read and react to signals from the leaders. They can't interpret the music as they hear it, even when their musical skills are better than the leader's. They aren't in charge, but they have the best time, whirling and relaxing and being dazzling."

I can see in Ruthie's face that she wants to be in control and she wants to be dazzling. She wants it all. Lawrence – well, he probably doesn't want any of it. He'd probably prefer to be behind the scenes.

"So you can see, it's about your individual personality, not whether you're a girl or boy. So what do you think? I'd like each of you, now, to tell me which role you think would work best for you."

I know what's going to happen before it happens, 'cause I've seen it a thousand times before. "He'll lead," Ruthie says, pointing at Lawrence.

"But what do *you* want to do, Ruthie?"

"Follow, of course."

"Why 'of course'?

"I'm the bride. It's my wedding." As usual, I've been wasting my time.

"What about you Lawrence? What would you prefer to do?"

He is an obedient and serious person – despite the head nodding all the time. "Well, according to what you're saying…" He switches his gaze from me to Ruthie and finishes his sentence towards her,

"You'd be the better leader."

"Okay, you two. Answer for yourselves, please, not for each other." I pick up the pitcher to re-fill it with chilled water in the kitchen, just off the living room. I am only a couple of yards away, but I suspect they need the illusion of privacy to work this out.

"I think I'd be a better follower than leader," he says.

"No, you wouldn't!" Here we go – I can hear fear and poison in Ruthie's voice.

"No, really. You know how I am. Like at work. I'm better in a support role than the head of something. In fact, I'd rather be the assistant director than be the director."

Ruthie's head swivels sideways. "You'd *what*?"

He flushes, nods, shakes his head – doesn't know what to do with himself. "Fred announced his resignation this morning. I thought about it all day. I'm not going to apply for his job. I prefer being where I am: the background guy."

Oh dear. These couples. Must they always tussle in my living room? I set down the pitcher in front of them and go back to my seat, saying, "Okay, I want to get started so I need your decisions." Ruthie ignores me. She's still on the subject of his job. She tugs at her shirt collar – this girl has more nervous habits than Red Skelton – and leans over, twisting so that her back is to me. She hisses right into Lawrence's face. "Don't you think this is something we ought to decide together?"

Lawrence is acutely aware of me. He leans away from Ruthie in order to pop out his head so that he can see me. "Excuse us for a minute. Sorry about this." He retracts his head back into her sight line.

He also whispers, "Let's discuss this at home."

"Will you lead?" She's a smart negotiator – get them when they're nervous.

"Sure."

At the end of the lesson, in which I show them the basic steps side-by side, we all open our datebooks and figure out our future schedule. That part is easier than I figured it would be, probably because she is anxious to leave so she can scold him for some mess-up at his job.

Whatever went on in their chat about Lawrence's career doesn't prevent them from coming back for every lesson. Along the way, Ruthie perfects what is known in partner dance as "back-leading." I don't much like this term, but in her case it does actually apply. She's leading from the position of the follower. She pulls Lawrence and pushes him and never waits for him to twirl her – she just does it herself when it's time. She counts them in at the beginning and times their final bow. He is in the mechanical position of a leader, but trust me, he is not leading.

Neither of them minds that, though. She wants the appearance to be right, damn the reality. She wants it to look like she is in the arms of a commanding man, so she leaves him to work on a commanding posture while she does the rest. Backwards. When I'm trying to show her something, she even tries to back-lead me. Meanwhile, it's very distracting to watch her pick at her waistband or adjust her sleeve cuffs, looking at me exasperated, even though I'm the professional and 50 years older than her. I don't think she likes anyone to know anything she doesn't know.

Like all my other matrimonial couples, Ruthie and Lawrence learn the routine by rote. Once they memorize the actual steps, I start to help them polish it. I get them to act out their poses and posture better. I'm not sure they realize that I'm teaching them performance more than real dance – so they'll look far more accomplished than they are. I give them arm flourishes and fake dips. Yeah, I pile it on, a bunch of dramatic gestures on top of simple footwork. Arm waves are cheap; footwork is hard, so I emphasize the trimmings. She's really good at illusion, but he is the better dancer. After six sessions, my job is done and the result is not half bad, so I send them off for their dance debut – less than a week away.

A couple of months later I receive in the mail a

video of their wedding that includes their triumphant meringue display, one that earns them a standing ovation from their guests. Ruthie has included a grateful, predictable note thanking me for being just the professional they needed in the run-up to their "jubilant ceremony."

Well, that's nice, I think. Good manners. Glad it was a success. But you know what? This couple – and they're not so different from some others I've worked with – this couple needed a professional all right, but not really a dance instructor: they needed a marriage counselor.

A couple of years pass. The transport van at our elder complex takes those of us who are mobile to our neighborhood's community fair. It's more crowded and noisy than I thought it would be so I'm trying to make my way through all the people to the café on the other end of the block where we're going to get picked up in an hour. But as I pass a band making such a racket up on a street stage, someone taps me on the shoulder. It's a man.

"I'm Lawrence," he screams over the music. Who is this guy? What's he want from me? "Who?" I shrug, trying to get past him.

"My fiancée Ruthie and I learned to dance with you before our wedding," he persists, leaning down and yelling in my ear.

Oh yeah. I remember then and nod. He too is nodding. Nodding and smiling and I can see something is different. Right. That missing tooth isn't missing anymore. So he got himself to a dentist. That's nice. He's looking better than the vague memory I have of him, cowering and pale.

But he won't let me go. He wants to tell me something. I look around for potential help, just in case he's lost his mind or something. "We divorced two months after marrying," he yells into my face. It comes flooding back. She was the back-leader.

Then he points to the drummer of the band. I follow his finger and see a woman in black leather and a hat like the jazz bands used to wear in the 40s – a pork pie. She's pounding with confidence on her drums. She looks powerful and calm. Despite the fact that she is trying to break my hearing aid – I'm so glad I turned it off – there's something nice about her.

He stares at the drummer with a big smile on his face. Well, well, I think. This guy has done more than fix his smile – he's gotten himself all happy. I notice that he's wearing a leather collar and that it has a well-worn ring in front. I wonder what it means when she looks down first really pointedly at his throat and then in his eyes. He flushes, but it's a good flush, not from high blood pressure or embarrassment. He's nodding his head to the music, which reminds me of how he nodded his head at everything his old fiancée had to say. His nodding doesn't seem odd anymore. This woman beats the drum and he quite happily follows her rhythm. I bet that if they decide to marry, she will lead the dance.

My Neighbor's Strange Attachment to the Cart

With such a racket in the hall, I can't help cracking open my door to peek. Movers are lugging a big table into the apartment across from mine. If you want to call these places in Windcrescent "apartments." The living room is all right, with plenty of windows. The bedroom holds a single bed and has a reasonable closet. The bathroom is tiny and disfigured by sickly pink tiling from the 70s. And if you call a toaster-oven and a burner a kitchen, well, then go ahead and call this an apartment. But my sister says I shouldn't complain since the town is subsidizing this building. "They don't want seniors living in the gutter and embarrassing the town," she says, never one to pass up a chance to try to make things political.

Even though she was a chain-smoker, I was sorry to see Emilia from across the hall go to the nursing home. Sorry for her and sorry for me. The rheumatoid arthritis got the better of her, I guess. I hope they figure out how to control her pain better than her own doctor did – or rather, didn't. Despite the cigarette stench in her clothes, her hair, and our hallway, she was quiet and she was polite. And she baked a mean almond cookie. Altogether, that made for a very nice neighbor.

Before I can duck back inside, I've been noticed by a nondescript smiling woman in her early 30s. Her hair is wilted and brown, much like the old-fashioned pleated skirt she's wearing.

"I'm Violet," she says, striding across the hall to shake my hand. I automatically give her my right hand, but with the left I pull my starched housedress more tightly closed at the neck. "My mother is moving in. I'll be here with her as much as possible, but I spend most of my time on the road. I'm in sales – dishwasher cleansers – and my region covers four states." She's clearly proud of her work, so I smile and try to shrink back inside. However, she walks backwards, returning to the open door of #810, gesturing for me to follow. She keeps what they call eye contact with me the whole time. I'm not wearing a bra or real shoes – just my fluffy slippers -- and would rather resume my work on the accounts I'm in the middle of preparing for a client. "Mama! Come meet the neighbor," she half-turns her head to shout into their apartment, without looking away from me.

I step into the hall reluctantly. She drags her mother by the hand towards me, introducing her as she does, but I can't catch the name. It's Reina or Rena or Rynah or something. She's younger than me, perhaps just in her mid 60s, but between the severe rounding of her back – osteoporosis? – and her meek demeanor, I can hardly hear her greeting.

"Welcome," I say. She looks up at me, expectantly. I'm not sure where to go from here. "It's a good location." I pause. Her expression stays the same. "Uh, the complex is well-built," I say, sounding to myself like an ad for municipal housing. But I guess that after seven years, I've become one of the old-timers. Still her head is bowed, her mouth is closed, and the daughter is staring at me encouragingly. I'm not a fan of awkward silences, so I point out a few of the building's highlights – the garbage closet, the mail chute, the emergency buttons in the living room and bathroom, the washer and dryer on every even-numbered floor, the elevators at the far end of the hall – all the time crossing my arms uncomfortably across my unsupported breasts.

My sister will have a good laugh over this, when I tell her. She's quit wearing bras altogether – and I've criticized her for it many a time. She says that old women are invisible anyway, so why not spend the final third of her life in complete comfort. Elastic waistbands and oversized cotton t-shirts are her religion, and to draw attention away from her flopping breasts, she had both her forearms tattooed, right after she qualified for Medicare about ten years ago. "Just in case of infection," she told me after turning 65, "I'm covered."

First she had her beloved peonies drawn on her

right arm. But she couldn't leave well enough alone. She had to add a quote from Ralph Waldo Emerson: *Earth laughs in flowers*. It's woven into the stems. "This is my optimistic arm," she told me, laughing, even though it was inflamed and ugly at first.

Less than a year later she declared her left arm the "militant" one and in square red letters wound around her forearm, she had them write *Women hold up half the sky*, a line from one of her favorite writers, Mao Tse-Tung. From China. When we go out together in the summer, I ask her to wear long sleeves. People must question whether we are really sisters, despite both of us having one ear so much bigger than the other.

The good daughter Violet plugs the silence. "Very useful info, isn't it Mama? Very useful."

The woman finally speaks for herself. "Yes, thank you, yes." She has spoken so few words that I can't identify what kind of accent she has. Not that I'm very good at recognizing foreign accents.

"And the transportation?" Violet asks, trying to keep the conversation sizzling.

I search my memory. Why don't they just read the brochure? "Well, I have my own car so I'm not sure of all the days, but the Windcrescent van goes to the supermarket and the drug store once a week, and, oh yes, to the Mall every Wednesday and Saturday."

Violet nods rigorously, smiling an oversized

smile. Her mother's still staring at the hall carpet. Now we're into another lull, and all I can think about is getting back to my bookkeeping task.

"Well, welcome to Windcrescent," I repeat, nodding, as I back up towards my own open door. That's about as intimate as I ever plan to get with, ah, we'll call her R. On this floor we neighbors rarely see each other, except for those awkward elevator encounters where observations about the weather or the terrible condition of our town's sidewalks accompany the rattles of ascent or descent.

I am, on this account, quite mistaken. Within her first week the saleswoman's mama seems to have fallen in love with one of the five shopping carts that live in the basement garage to provide temporary assistance with hauling shopping and whatnot up to our apartments. They are lined up under a handwritten sign: "Please return the cart immediately for the convenience of others." R. seems to have become as one with one of the carts. Every day, and often more than once, I hear it rattling out of the elevator at the far end of the hall, bumping through the double doors, and rolling up the hall to her apartment, across from mine. It's a noise one doesn't mind once or twice a week, but it gets on my nerves when it's every day. How many groceries can one woman buy?

And she leaves this shopping cart all over the

place. Now, when I go out of my place I inevitably find it obstructing my passage down to the double doors that lead to the elevator, the laundry, and the garbage closet. Sometimes when I'm returning home, I come out of the elevator and the cart is blocking my way. I've had my bag snagged by it, my hipbone knocked by it.

But that's not the worst part. I'm concerned about safety, frankly. I'm big on safety. My sister says I'm neurotic, but she doesn't live in an apartment building. I've always lived in them, so I have that flat-dweller fear of fire. All it takes is one drunk to fall asleep with a cigarette in hand – which happened at the last place I lived and he was the superintendent – or one old person with memory troubles to forget about the bubbling frying pan. I read about these infernos all the time. You see it on the news too often. So I get nervous when she parks the cart across the bottom of the stairwell, which is where I'm supposed to flee if there's a fire. They turn off the elevator. It says that right on the elevator wall. 'Take the stairs in case of an emergency.'

"But what is she doing with the cart?" I ask my sister. "Surely she can't be hauling that much shopping every day."

"Sounds like romance," my sister jokes. "Sounds like she's become attached to the metal mesh, to the rickety wheels, to that deep, gaping basket." The way she draws out "deep, gaping basket" makes me blush.

She does this to embarrass me. My sister sexualizes things; she's provocative. She considers herself poetic. That's probably the point she's trying to establish with those tattoos.

Anyway, a day or two later, all is revealed. It turns out that it isn't shopping that my neighbor is doing. It's laundry. All day, all night, she's got our community washing machine and dryer going. She's rude about it, too. She does a load and just leaves it in the washer for a long time while I'm waiting to do my own laundry. I leave a note, anonymously of course, outlining proper behavior vis-à-vis the shared washer. "Remove your clothes from the machine in a timely manner."

As for the dryer, after a detailed note I tape to the dryer's control panel, she begins attempting to clean the lint filter, but unfortunately she stuffs the mesh filter back into its slot upside down, damaging the screen. I tape up more extensive instructions, but she still fails to figure it out.

I hate to sound like the bookkeeper I am, but the issue is a quantitative one as much as a qualitative one. How much laundry can one woman do? How can she be up and down the hall with a cartload of washing at least every day, if not several times a day? Maybe the daughter, whom I have never seen again, drops her laundry by. But then how many times a day does a salesperson on the road change her clothes? I discuss the matter with my sister, who suggests that R. is running a laundry business.

"Unlikely," I tell her, "Not at $1.50 to wash and $1.50 to dry. Not really a business model that could work."

"I've figured it out," she cries. "She's incontinent." My sister was a nurse's aide.

Where fire had been my big concern about Emilia, the smoker who moved out, I find my sister's suggestion about this particular neighbor more than sobering. I'm embarrassed to admit this idea is repugnant to me. We shouldn't really hold health problems against the sufferer. I do know that. But what can I do? I'd like to be more generous in my thoughts than I am, but it apparently doesn't come as easy to me as it does to my sister. I begin to be haunted by unwelcome images of my own clothes swirling around a machine drenched in her urine.

In my too-frequent encounters with R. and her sidekick cart in the hall, she increasingly becomes talkative and asks me questions I don't have answers for. What do I think of the new guy down the hall? I tell her I've only seen him once and I don't think anything one way or another. But don't I agree that he receives a suspicious number of packages? I am disturbed by her nosiness and insist

I know nothing about it. One day she hones in on me, crowding me with the cart and looking up at me with eyes that are oddly shiny: Where do I go when I leave so early in the morning on Wednesdays? I go out, I scowl.

This is senior housing. We all rent. It's not a neighborhood square or a homeowners association. People give and expect the kind of privacy that might not feel neighborly to people used to owning adjoining homes or even condos that are next to each other. There is a code of rental conduct to which R. seems oblivious.

As the weeks pass, she becomes ever more emboldened, leaving her beloved shopping cart in the middle of the hall where it's a danger to the old people down at the other end and a barrier to quick escape for all of us. It's becoming a permanent fixture: either it's sitting there awaiting her or she's pushing the thing up or down the hall. Occasionally I am stranded behind her as she lumbers along.

"Maybe it's serving her as some kind of walker," my sister the health professional suggests in her superior tone. The implication is that I'm an impatient able-bodied person, at best. "Maybe you're right," I reply, quashing a lifetime of feeling defensive. But what does my sister know about these things? She has her own little cottage, way outside town. "I'd rather have my own four walls and miss a few exhibitions and concerts" – she doesn't drive – "than live like one of your aged sardines," she's said more than once.

"Well, what do you make of this?" I ask my sister next time she calls. "How's this for bizarre behavior?" My neighbor, I tell her, now actually stands guard when she is running the washer or dryer. She hovers with the lights off just behind the door of the laundry room – opposite the elevator – so that one cannot leave or arrive without her taking a rather creepy notice.

This shuts my sister up. So I persist, feeling I am gaining the advantage. "What is the point of guarding a washing machine or dryer on your own floor in your own apartment house? Does she think people are after her foundation garments – pee-soaked or not? Does she worry people will pinch her towels?"

My sister is thinking. I can tell from the silence down the line. "Didn't you say she had an accent? Maybe that's how they do it where she comes from and we just don't understand." She is clutching at straws, my sister is, and I say goodbye with no small satisfaction.

But I hadn't been totally open with my sister concerning what really bothers me about this situation. I have never been able to imagine what people do who just sit or stand in a place – no book or knitting or notebook in hand. I can't even understand beach holidays or sunbathing afternoons, but at least there's comfort and beauty. Day after day, load of fabric after load, what is going through R.'s mind as she stands, just out of sight behind the doorjamb, doing nothing?

I get pretty steamed, one day, when a visitor of mine gets her cane caught and stumbles over the cart R. has left just outside the elevator door. Does R. not know what a door is? It's something we go in and out of. Why park an awkward cart right there? I can't hold my tongue any longer.

I settle my friend in a comfortable chair in my apartment and go back up the hall to the laundry room where R. is lurking, almost hidden. When I stick my head around the door and snap on the light, she tenses. I tell her she should not be leaving the shopping cart in common space. I explain that obstructions of shared areas need to be avoided. I can't read her face or her reaction – her head is bowed. She's probably one of those people who lived in a private house all their lives and think of the hall and the garbage area and the laundry as an extension of their own living area. They even leave their front door open to the hall, as R. sometimes does, forcing the sounds of their life and the smells of their food on unwilling neighbors. That's wrong. It gets me riled up. These oblivious homeowners, I boil, they take liberties. R. is unresponsive and I don't want to leave my poor guest alone too long, so I turn and return home up the hall.

Another time, I'm going away for a long weekend with my sister. I load my shoulder purse, my carry-bag of board games, and my travel bag over my shoulders. In one hand I carry the insulated refrigerator bag with my meatloaf and a fruit salad, and in the other I hold a final sack of garbage to deposit in the garbage room on my way out. I clump down the hall and turn my back to use my shoulder to push open the double doors. The large glass panel of the door slams against the handle of an unseen shopping cart that R. has parked out of sight, half in and half out of the laundry room.

My heart shudders at the collision, reverberating around my chest. To my horror, the bag with my meatloaf escapes my grasp and crashes onto the floor. R. is wrestling with the cart and I am still on the wrong side of the double doors. When she clears the way I push the door open and say with not insignificant heat, "You're putting the rest of us in danger. Quit leaving the carts where people walk. Stop it!"

She pulls the cart into the laundry room and I can't see her. I'm too encumbered to chase her in there so, fuming, I get onto the elevator and leave. When I get downstairs I realize that I'm still clutching my garbage bag. For my own peace of mind, I do not tell my sister about this incident. I doubt that whatever she has to say about my outburst will benefit my mood.

On my return four days later, R. is nowhere to be seen. The machines on our floor are not being operated day and night. I do not see her in the hall, although I hear her rattling along with the cart at least two or three times a day. I start to have a guilt attack – I picture her bent over and cowering in the far corner of her flat.

This situation is a constant niggling worry in the back of my mind, especially as I haven't talked it through with my sister. Have I done wrong? This neighbor scared me and I reacted. My back was up against the glass when it struck the metal of the cart – that could have been disastrous. She had already annoyed me day after day with her appropriation of all that should be shared. She disregarded everyone else's safety. I had every right to speak sharply to her. Didn't I?

She seems to have evaporated. I never see her in the halls when I go in or out. I wonder where she is and if I have made her life a misery. I fantasize that she is sorry she ever moved here and is living in paranoid hell – and I certainly wouldn't want to be the source of that misery. I remember a time when I cried and cried for weeks because of something mean a colleague had said to me (he didn't even remember the incident when I remarked on it months later) – and I wouldn't wish that kind of angst on anyone. I try to think up excuses to make contact, but I know better than to set a precedent of knocking on her door. I haven't even seen the daughter since moving day, either. Weeks pass.

One day I leave my apartment and as I make my way down the hall I see a cart being pulled into the laundry room just as the light in the room is turned off. I go right in and there she is, huddling over the cart against the far wall of the laundry. I turn the light back on. "What are you doing?" I ask, but gently.

"Keeping out of your way." She says this, not in her usual murmuring way, but with a fierce resentment and exaggerated sarcasm, curling her lip and looking up at me with scorn.

Her unexpected growling tone puts me on the defensive. "You put the cart where the glass of the door would hit it. That was dangerous."

"That was not," she leans her upper body toward me, sneering, "my intention."

She is glaring at me. I'm not sure what comes next. "And it wasn't my intention to make you hide," I say in a conciliatory voice. So she hasn't been a miserable puddle – she's been a cauldron of fury.

Without warning, she thrusts out her hand, reaching over the cart. "Friends?" she asks in a bewildering switch.

I shake her hand, but I want to be clear. "Good neighbors," I smile. Then I shake her hand again, just to let her know that I consider this a good thing.

I get in the elevator relieved that I can dump that sense of guilt, but feeling creeped out. Something is very weird about all of this. My stomach is acidy and my brow somewhat damp. I call my sister from the car. From the emotion in my voice, she knows something is up. "Pull over," she says. "You shouldn't drive and hold the phone, especially when you're talking about something intense. I'm hanging up for the moment." And she does.

I pull into the CVS parking lot and call her back. I pour out the whole story, including the fact that I haven't been keeping her up-to-date. I tell her how disturbed I feel, perhaps even more so to discover this hard side of the woman's personality.

My sister, for once, knows just what I mean. "But how did she avoid you for so long?" she wonders. "How did she always know when you were coming and going? It's like she put some microphone on your door or a hidden camera in the hall."

My sister's rare sympathy doesn't really help me. Instead, she has planted those images in my mind and they haunt me every time I go in or out of my apartment door. Even when I'm inside, just living my life in the quiet manner that suits me, I feel disconcerted. I sense R. and her cart right across the hall, knowing something and feeling something I cannot fathom.

This morning I open my door and look down the hall before walking to the far end in my housedress to dispose of a bag of garbage. Just as I am returning, R.'s daughter Violet comes out of the elevator. We recognize each other even though it's only our second meeting. "Well hello," she says with an open smile, "How nice to see you again."

I nod, self-consciously crossing my arms.

"And hey, thanks so much for being such a generous neighbor to my mother. Whenever she complains that I never visit, she sighs and says, 'I am lucky to at least have fine neighbors.'" I search her face for any indication of sarcasm, but there is none. She goes into her mother's door with a happy wave and, embarrassed, I slip inside my own apartment to call my sister.

30857480R00082

Made in the USA
Charleston, SC
28 June 2014